The Forger's Den

MONUMENTAL BOOKS

The Adventures Of Boubou & Aya : Volume 3
The Forger's Den
by Walter Simin

Published by Monumental Books

3 rue de Turbigo
75001 Paris
France

www.waltersimin.com

For permission requests, contact: info@monumentalstudio.com

Layout and book distribution by Monumental Books

Printed in 2024

ISBN:
978-2-487769-05-2 (hardcover)
978-2-487769-04-5 (paperback)
978-2-487769-03-8 (ebook)

First Edition

EDUCATIONAL RESOURCES

Dear Parents, Teachers, and Educators,

If you're considering "Boubou & Aya: The Forger's Den" for educational purposes, or are already using it in your curriculum, we invite you to enhance your experience with our complimentary educational package. Tailored to complement the themes and adventures of the book, this resource is designed to deepen understanding and engagement for young readers.

This dynamic package includes a variety of activities and materials: from reading comprehension quizzes and cultural exploration activities to creative writing prompts and detective skill-building exercises. It's an excellent tool to foster discussion, enhance vocabulary, and encourage a deeper appreciation of the story's themes such as family, courage, and cultural diversity.

We believe that this package will not only support your teaching goals but also enrich the reading experience, making it more interactive and enjoyable. Whether in a classroom, homeschooling environment, or any other educational setting, these resources are here to help you bring the magic of "Boubou & Aya" to life.

www.waltersimin.com/downloads/

Enjoy the journey of learning and adventure!

ACKNOWLEDGEMENTS

To my dear cousin Dominique, this book is dedicated to you, my
partner in crime and adventure during those golden summers at our
grandparents' lakehouse. Remember how we'd spend countless hours
exploring every nook and cranny of the forest? We were two young
explorers, risking life and limb as we climbed trees, built
rickety rafts, and ventured into uncharted territory.

You were there for every scraped knee, every triumphant catch,
every whispered secret. Our adventures shaped who I am today and
inspired the very essence of Boubou and Aya's journey. In many
ways, this book series is a tribute to our childhood escapades and the
unbreakable bond we forged amidst nature's playground. My dear
cousin, this one's for you. For the summers we shared, the adventures
we braved, and the friendship that has stood the test of time.
I love you, couz.

With a heart full of nostalgia and gratitude,

Walter Simin

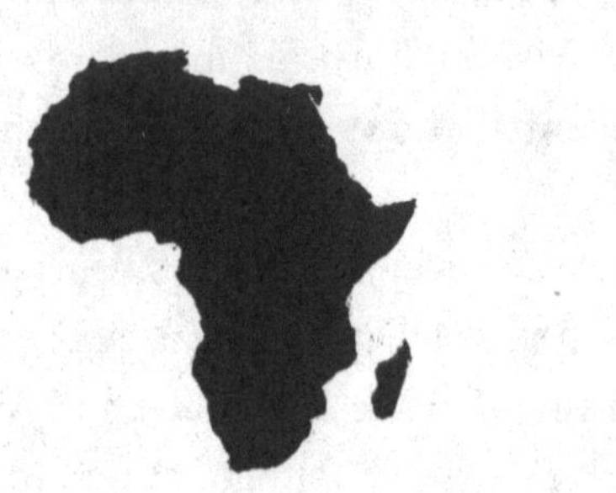

THE ADVENTURES OF
BOUBOU & AYA

The Forger's Den

WALTER SIMIN

Contents

CHAPTER ONE

A Swindler On The Train

THE AFTERNOON EXPRESS THUNDERED INTO ZINGUICHOU station, bringing with it a whirlwind of noise and activity. The air buzzed with clanging bells from the station café, shouts from porters, and the booming voice of the train announcer echoing off the walls.

On the bustling platform, Boubou and Aya Diouf stood out from the sea of passengers. The teen siblings, with friendly faces and eyes full of excitement, scanned the parade of train cars for a familiar face.

"I don't see her anywhere," Boubou, the older brother, said as he peered into another coach.

"Maybe it was too crowded, and she took the ferry instead?" Aya suggested, hopefully. "It's only an hour behind, right?"

They kept watching the stream of people, waiting for their grandmother to appear. After losing their parents – their dad, the famous detective Malik Diouf, and their mom – in a mysterious car crash a few years ago, Grandma Diouf had become their guardian. She'd been away in Zakar dealing with family stuff and was supposed to come home today.

As the last passengers trickled off the train, their hopes started to fade. There was no sign of Grandma Diouf.

"I guess we should check the ferry," Boubou sighed.

Just as they were about to leave, a tall, well-dressed stranger caught their eye. He was in his thirties, with dark features and a clean-shaven face. He walked up to them confidently, but there was something mysterious about him.

"I'll give anyone $5 from this," the stranger said, waving a $50 bill. "Got any change? I owe my buddy $20, and he's waiting for me right now."

He was charming and clearly in a hurry.

"I could try the station café, but it's a madhouse in there. It'd take forever to get someone's attention," the man explained, the bill fluttering between his fingers.

Boubou glanced at Aya and started digging through his pockets. "I've got $20 on me, Aya. What about you?"

Aya pulled out her wallet and counted. "I've got $10.53," she said. "So that's $30.53 total. Not enough."

"No worries!" The stranger handed his $50 bill to Boubou, who gave the man his $20 and Aya's $10.53.

"Thanks so much," the young man grinned. "You just saved me a ton of time and trouble. Plus, you made $18.47 for yourselves. Pretty clever, you two! Gotta run, though. This isn't my final stop, and I promised my friend I'd pay him back before we leave. Thanks again!"

Boubou shrugged casually, tucking the bill into his pocket. "No problem," he said. "Thanks to you too. Have a safe trip."

The man nodded gratefully, still smiling as he hurried back onto the train with a relaxed wave goodbye.

Aya watched him go, looking thoughtful. "It feels good to help someone out, doesn't it?"

"Yeah, and it was lucky I had the cash. Grandma gave me some money to buy spices for dinner tonight."

"Spices!" Aya's face lit up like a firecracker. "I mean, what's better than a whole bunch of new spices marching into our kitchen? More spices means more of Grandma's legendary meals!"

Grandma had a magical touch with spices, the secret superstars of African cooking. In her kitchen, colorful jars of spices lined the shelves like tasty treasures. Every dish she made showed off her skills: cumin added warmth, coriander brought a lemony zing, and chili peppers gave everything a spicy kick. She knew exactly how to mix these flavors to make meals that were more than just food – they were like a dance party for your taste buds! Her cooking wasn't just yummy; it was like taking a trip through all the amazing flavors of African food traditions. In every pot and pan, Grandma's spices told stories of family, community, and the heart and soul of African cooking.

"We should probably go buy those spices before I forget," Boubou said. "There's a little shop just down the street. We can get what we need, break this $50 bill, and kill some time before the ferry gets here."

They left the station and stepped out onto Zinguichou's main street, bathed in warm summer sunshine. Boubou and Aya were your typical high school kids, full of energy and well-known around town. Boubou, three years older, was tall and skinny, while Aya was shorter and had a mop of wild, curly hair. They waved and said hi to several people they knew as they walked.

Just as they were getting close to the spice shop, they heard the train whistle blow and the loud clang of the bell as the express started moving again, heading south.

"Looks like our new friend's trip will be smooth sailing now," Boubou joked. "He managed to break his $50 after all."

"And that other guy got his $20," Aya added. "I guess everybody wins!"

Approaching the store, they paused momentarily outside, their eyes caught by an array of football shoes on display. They debated over the studs' quality and the weights, contrasting them with their own well-worn, battle-scarred balls back home. Boubou and Aya cherished their after-school and weekend football matches with friends. In their community, football wasn't just a sport; it was a passion that brought everyone together. The dusty fields would come alive with shouts and laughter as they played, the sun setting a golden backdrop. For Boubou, Aya, and their friends, these moments were about more than just the game; they were a celebration of camaraderie, a testament to the sport's unifying power. In Africa, where football reigns supreme, these games were a cherished ritual, a shared joy that transcended the mere kicking of a ball. It was about teamwork, resilience, and the pure, unadulterated joy of playing the game they all loved.

After a while, they drifted inside, where they were welcomed by Moumba, the shop's owner. He was a pleasantly plump and cheerful fellow, lounging against the counter, engrossed in the day's paper. The shop was quiet, a lull in the day's business.

"Here to solve another mystery?" Moumba quipped, putting aside his newspaper as the Diouf siblings entered.

Being the children of Malik Diouf, and quite the budding detectives themselves, Boubou and Aya were often the target of friendly jokes about their detective escapades. They always took these jests in stride, understanding the light-hearted intent behind them.

"No clues to be found here," Mr. Moumba continued with a twinkle in his eye. "Not a single one. Just yesterday, I had a whole crate of top-notch bank robbery clues, but they were all snatched up. Expecting a fresh batch of murder clues tomorrow morning, if you're willing to wait. Or maybe I should place an order for some kidnapping clues for you? Size eight and a half, long-lasting and with a no-fade guarantee."

Mr. Moumba carried on, his voice dripping with mock seriousness. He suddenly burst into a hearty laugh at his own jest, swinging his legs playfully against the counter.

"So, what's it going to be, kids?" he asked, wiping tears of laughter from his eyes, as Boubou and Aya grinned back.

"We're here for spices," Aya said with a smile. "For Grandma. Three hundred grams."

"Ah, not the overly spicy ones, right?" Mr. Moumba teased, his chuckle booming through the shop as the siblings gave him a mock-indignant look.

"Quite the opposite," Boubou retorted. "We want the spiciest you've got!"

Mr. Moumba, laughing heartily at their response, swung around from the counter and went to fetch the spices. He knew exactly what their Grandma usually bought. Returning, he carefully measured out the spices, ensuring they were just right.

"Let's wrap these up," Boubou said, placing the five-thousand franc note on the counter.

As Mr. Moumba wrapped the spices, he picked up the note and walked over to the cash register. He was about to complete the transaction when he paused, holding the note up to the light. He rubbed it between his fingers, feeling its texture, his eyes closely examining every detail.

"Where did this note come from, kids?" Mr. Moumba asked, his tone shifting to one of concern.

"Oh, we just swapped it for a guy we met on the train," Boubou replied, a hint of confusion in his voice. "Is there something wrong with it?"

Mr. Moumba examined the note with a skeptical eye. "This looks fishy to me. I can't risk accepting it, I'm afraid."

He handed the note back to Boubou, then gestured towards the spices on the counter.

"What's the plan for these spices, then?" he inquired. "Got any other cash besides this note?"

"Not even a dime," Aya chimed in. "Well, not enough for the spices, anyway. But are you sure there's something off with this note?"

"I've seen plenty of these in my time, and this one doesn't seem right. Here's what you should do: take it to the bank right across the street. See what the cashier has to say about it."

The realization of what this might mean hit the siblings like a ton of bricks. The thought that the note could be counterfeit and that they might have been duped by the friendly stranger had never crossed their minds. But now, doubt crept in.

"Alright, we'll do just that," Boubou agreed, a determined look on his face. "Let's go, Aya. Mr. Moumba, could you hold onto the spices for us? If this note's a dud, we'll come back with some genuine cash later."

❖

Boubou and Aya hurried across the street to the bank. They were pretty well-known there, thanks to their incredible adventures. For kids their age, they had a lot of money saved up. They'd been rewarded by the Countess for finding her stolen diamonds in the Lighthouse robbery and again for helping catch the Scorpion, the scary leader of a gang that smuggled illegal diamonds.

The bank teller, who knew all about the siblings' exciting life, smiled as Boubou slid the $50 bill through the window.

"Well, hello there, my young detective friends!" he said cheerfully. "Need some change today?"

"Actually, we need to know if it's real," Boubou replied.

"Yeah, we think we might have been tricked," Aya added, frowning.

The teller, Mr. Sousou, was an older man with a sharp face and glasses. He looked at the bill very carefully, feeling the paper. After a moment, his face got serious, and he slid the bill back to them.

"I'm sorry to tell you this, kids, but this is fake," he said sadly.

"Fake!" Boubou gasped, shocked.

Aya's eyes widened in disbelief. "No way! Are you absolutely sure, Mr. Sousou?"

"I'm afraid so, Aya," Mr. Sousou replied gently. "You're not the only ones. There's been a lot of fake money going around lately. It's so well-made that it can fool anyone who doesn't handle money all day long. Where did you get it?"

"Well, we were at the train station waiting for our grandmother," Boubou began.

"And this guy came up to us, all charming and in a hurry," Aya said.

"Yeah," Boubou continued, "he said he needed change for a $50 bill. Said he owed his friend $10."

"We thought we were being helpful!" Aya exclaimed. "We even made some money on the deal."

Boubou shook his head. "Or so we thought. He seemed so nice and grateful."

Mr. Sousou nodded, a look of recognition crossing his face. "I see. I hate to say it, but this sounds familiar. Go on."

"That's pretty much it," Boubou shrugged. "He thanked us and rushed back onto the train."

"Probably to go trick someone else at the next stop," Aya added sarcastically.

Mr. Sousou sighed. "I'm afraid you might be right, Aya. That's exactly how these scammers operate. They rely on people's kindness and rush them so they don't have time to think."

"Man, I can't believe we fell for it," Boubou said, his shoulders slumping.

Aya rolled her eyes. "Some detectives we are, huh?"

"Don't be too hard on yourselves," Mr. Sousou reassured them. "Like I said, these counterfeiters are getting very good at what they do."

"I can't believe this!" Aya exploded, her face turning red. "That sneaky, no-good... ugh! We were trying to help him, and he totally played us!"

"Aya, calm down," Boubou said, putting a hand on her shoulder.

"Calm down? We just lost fifty bucks, Boubou!" Aya fumed. "And Grandma's spices! What are we going to tell her?"

Mr. Sousou gave them a sympathetic look. "I'm afraid you'll have to count this as a loss, kids. It's not fair, but these things happen sometimes."

"Well, it shouldn't happen!" Aya huffed, crossing her arms. "When I get my hands on that guy..."

"Aya," Boubou warned, then turned to Mr. Sousou. "Thanks for your help, sir. We appreciate it."

As they turned to leave, Aya muttered, "Next time someone asks me for change, I'm gonna look them dead in the eye and say, 'Do I look like a bank to you?'"

CHAPTER TWO

Faux Dollars and Family Ties

Boubou and Aya burst out of the bank, their faces mixed with embarrassment and anger.

"We've been totally scammed!" Boubou groaned, throwing his hands up. "If our friends ever find out about this, we'll never hear the end of it!"

Aya's eyes narrowed. "That sneaky trickster probably thinks he's so clever. I bet he's still laughing about how easy it was to fool us!"

"We walked right into it," Boubou sighed, shaking his head. "Talk about gullible!"

"Well, you've got to admit," Aya said, trying to find a silver lining, "that fake bill could've fooled almost anyone. It looks just like a real fifty-dollar note!"

They stopped at the street corner and studied the counterfeit money again. It was crisp and new, a near-perfect copy of the real thing.

"You know," Aya muttered, "if we weren't such goody-two-shoes, we could probably pass this off to someone else." She frowned. "But what a rotten way to learn not to trust strangers! That crook is probably doing a victory dance right now."

Boubou's stomach growled loudly. "It's not just about getting tricked," he grumbled. "This was supposed to pay for our dinner tonight. Looks like we're having air sandwiches instead!"

Aya's eyes widened as the full impact of their situation hit her. They hadn't just been fooled – they were now broke and starving!

"Great," she mumbled. "We've gone from suckers to hungry suckers. What a day!"

❖

Boubou and Aya trudged back to Mr. Moumba's store, their faces as long as a summer's day. The shopkeeper raised an eyebrow, already guessing what they were about to say.

"It was fake," Boubou mumbled, scuffing his shoe on the floor. "The bank teller took one look and knew right away."

Mr. Moumba's face softened. "Ah, that's rough, kids. But I'm glad I spotted it. In this business, you've got to have eyes like a hawk!" He leaned in, lowering his voice dramatically. "Actually, I might've been fooled too if the bank hadn't warned me this morning about a bunch of funny money going around."

He tapped his nose knowingly. "When I saw how crisp your bill was, my merchant's instinct kicked in. Whoever's making these is no backyard counterfeiter – they're the real deal at making fake deals!"

"We'll be back for the spices once we figure this out," Boubou promised. "We just didn't want you thinking we were trying to pull a fast one on you."

Mr. Moumba burst out laughing, his belly shaking like a bowl full of jelly. "The Diouf duo, criminal masterminds? Ha! I'd sooner believe my cat could fly!" He wiped a tear from his eye. "Don't sweat the spices, kids. I'll set them aside, or you can take them now and pay me later. Just make sure it's the genuine article next time!" He wagged his finger at them, his eyes twinkling with mischief.

"We'll be back before you know it," they chorused, their spirits lifting a little. At least someone still believed in them!

As they left the store, Aya whispered to Boubou, "Well, that went better than expected. Think he'd notice if we paid him in Monopoly money next time?"

Boubou groaned. "Aya! Don't even joke about that!"

Boubou and Aya slumped onto a bench at the ferry station, waiting for their grandmother to arrive. The bustling crowd around them did nothing to lift their gloomy mood.

"It's not even about the thirty bucks," Boubou grumbled. "It's how we fell for such a basic trick! That guy had plenty of places to change his money – the café, newsstand, ticket office. But no, we just handed ours over like total rookies—"

"Well, sheep don't have pockets," Aya quipped, a tiny smirk breaking through her frown.

Despite their frustration, Aya's silly comment made Boubou chuckle. Even when things went wrong, they still had each other's backs.

"Maybe it's better sheep don't have pockets," Boubou mused. "They'd probably end up like us – tricked and broke!"

Aya nodded, her face turning serious again. "We didn't even look at that bill closely. I feel like I need a time-out for being so gullible."

As they sat there feeling sorry for themselves, the irony wasn't lost on either of them. Here they were, the kids of Africa's most famous detective, and they'd fallen for one of the oldest tricks in the book! The thought of explaining this to their grandmother, who was due any minute, made them both want to disappear.

But beneath their embarrassment, a determination was growing. This experience, as awful as it felt, was a valuable lesson. It reminded them that even the smartest people can be fooled and that you must always stay on your toes. It was a lesson they wouldn't forget anytime soon.

Boubou and Aya grew up in Zinguichou, a beautiful city by the ocean where the Cazamoun River flows. Their dad, Malik Diouf, was a super-famous private investigator. He used to be a top cop in Dakar but retired early to solve tricky cases all over Africa.

Malik, his wife Lika, and the kids had chosen Zinguichou because it was peaceful and pretty. The city had about two thousand people, and it was the perfect place for the Dioufs to have a normal family life when Malik wasn't out catching bad guys. Boubou and Aya went to school there and loved exploring the city's culture and nature.

Now in high school, both siblings knew how amazing their dad was. His detective stories weren't just bedtime tales – they were real adventures! Even though their mom, Lika, hoped they'd choose safer jobs, Boubou and Aya dreamed of being detectives like their dad. They loved the excitement and brain-teasers that came with solving mysteries.

Boubou remembered a conversation from last year:

"But Mom," he had protested, "being an accountant sounds so… boring!"

Lika had sighed, shaking her head. "Boring pays the bills, sweetie. And accountants don't get shot at."

"Yeah, but do they get to crack secret codes or chase bad guys?" Aya had chimed in, her eyes sparkling with excitement.

"No," their mom had admitted, "but they also don't give their poor mothers heart attacks every other week."

Aya recalled another time when she'd tried to explain their passion:

"It's like the best puzzle ever, Mom!" she'd exclaimed. "Every clue is a piece, and when you put them all together—"

"You get a big target on your back," Lika had finished, but there was a hint of a smile on her face.

"Come on, Mom," Boubou had added. "Dad always said the biggest thrill was outsmarting the criminals, not outrunning them."

Their mom had just rolled her eyes, but they could tell she was fighting back a proud grin. "You two are too much like your father for your own good," she'd said, ruffling their hair affectionately.

Those memories made Boubou and Aya smile, even as they sat on the ferry station bench. Sure, being a detective was risky, but to them, it was the most exciting job in the world.

Growing up this way made them proud of their dad, but it also made them want to fight for justice and truth. They still had a lot to learn – getting tricked by that fake money was proof of that! But they were determined to follow in their dad's footsteps, no matter how tough it got.

Boubou and Aya had already solved two big mysteries in Zinguichou, showing they had their dad's talent for detective work.

As Boubou and Aya sat on the ferry station bench, memories of their past adventures flashed through their minds. They couldn't help but feel a bit embarrassed about falling for such a simple trick, especially given their track record.

"Remember when we cracked 'The Lighthouse Mystery'?" Boubou whispered, trying to boost their spirits. "We found those stolen diamonds and that weird golden beetle statue when even the police were clueless."

Aya nodded, a small smile playing on her lips. "And don't forget 'The Fisherman's Fortune' case. That was way tougher than some guy with fake money."

"True," Boubou agreed. "We uncovered a whole smuggling ring right under everyone's noses. Even rescued Chief Gaye from that creepy Scorpion guy."

"The police had been chasing their tails for years on that one," Aya added, her confidence returning a bit.

They both chuckled, remembering the wild chase through Kambossa's cliffside house that had wrapped up their last big case. After that, they'd enjoyed a pretty quiet summer filled with lazy days by the river and hanging out with friends.

"Maybe we got too comfortable," Boubou mused. "Started to think we were unbeatable or something."

Aya sighed. "I guess even junior detectives can have off days. But next time..." Her eyes narrowed with determination. "Next time, we'll be ready."

The siblings shared a knowing look. They might have stumbled today, but their past successes reminded them of what they were capable of. Whatever mystery came their way next, they'd face it head-on – older, wiser, and more cautious than ever. They hung out with friends, played tons of soccer, and had fun by the Cazamoun River near Zabrousse. It was nice to relax after all their detective work.

But as the rainy season ended and warm weather returned, Boubou and Aya had a feeling new mysteries were just around the corner. Their natural curiosity and growing detective skills meant it was only a matter of time before they stumbled into another puzzling situation.

The siblings felt extra annoyed about being tricked because they were usually so good at solving mysteries. It felt like a big mark against their detective record.

"Dad would have a field day with this one," Aya sighed as they heard the ferry's whistle in the distance.

"We should still tell him about it during our next clairvoyant session with Grandma," Boubou said, trying to be positive. "Who knows? Maybe this mess could lead us to an even bigger case!"

Their grandmother was famous in Zinguichou for being able to talk to spirits. She helped the kids connect with their dad, who had passed away. Through her, they often asked their father for advice, which helped them solve many cases. This special connection not only gave them great insights but also made them feel close to their dad.

Aya especially loved these sessions. Being able to reach out to their parents made her feel less sad about losing them. It was a unique part of their lives that mixed magic with detective work, giving them a unique advantage and helping them deal with tough situations. After their counterfeit money disaster, their grandmother's spiritual skills seemed more important than ever. It wasn't just about getting advice – it was a chance to understand and learn from their mistakes.

❖

As the ferry docked, Grandma Diouf appeared like a burst of color in her bright, hand-made dress. Her gray hair sparkled in the sun, and even at seventy, she moved with the energy of someone half her age. When she spotted Boubou and Aya, her face lit up like a fireworks display.

"There are my favorite junior detectives!" she called out, wrapping them in a big, warm hug that smelled like cinnamon and home.

"Hi, Grandma," Boubou mumbled into her shoulder, secretly loving the fuss.

Grandma Diouf held them at arm's length, her eyes twinkling. "So, what kind of mischief have you two been stirring up?"

Aya shuffled her feet. "Well, we've been mischief-free... but trouble found us anyway."

"Oh?" Grandma's eyebrows shot up. "Spill the beans, kids."

"Remember that special dinner you mentioned?" Aya started, her voice small. "We, uh, kind of lost the spice money to a guy with fake cash."

Grandma listened, her face a mix of 'Oh no' and 'Tell me more.'

"How in the world did that happen?" she asked, eyes wide.

Boubou sighed. "This guy came up, all friendly, asking to break a fifty-dollar bill."

"Ah," Grandma nodded, "and then what?"

"Turns out, it was as fake as a three-dollar bill," Aya finished.

Grandma's face turned serious. "Do you still have it?"

"Right here," Boubou said, carefully handing over the bogus bill. "We couldn't tell, Grandma. It looks so real!"

Grandma examined the bill closely, then tucked it into her purse. "I'll hang onto this," she said, leading them away from the dock. "This isn't just any counterfeit, you know."

"What do you mean?" Boubou asked, suddenly curious.

"Well," Grandma said, lowering her voice, "I'm not saying I know this exact bill's story, but your dad was working on a case just like this before he passed. The government had asked him to help take down a big counterfeiting ring."

"Whoa, really?" Aya's eyes were as big as saucers.

Grandma's eyes twinkled with mischief. "Tell you what – let's grab those spices, head home, and I'll tell you all about it over a special ritual. Maybe your dad will have some clues to share from the great beyond."

"That's awesome, Grandma!" Boubou grinned, suddenly feeling much better about their day.

Boubou and Aya shared an excited look as they headed to Mr. Moumba's shop. Their adventure was just beginning!

❖

Back home, Boubou and Aya sat cross-legged on the floor, eyes glued to Grandma Diouf's old woven tray. The room was dim and cozy, like something out of a mystery movie. Grandma arranged her shiny cowrie shells, each one looking like a tiny, magical pearl. She tossed them onto the tray, and suddenly, the shells became a secret code only she could read.

As Grandma started chanting softly, the room got super quiet. The air felt thick with excitement. Boubou and Aya leaned in close, their faces lit up by flickering candles and curiosity. They were dying to know what the shells would reveal about their weird day.

Grandma's voice was as smooth as honey when she spoke. "Your dad's spirit is worried," she said, still staring at the shells. "He says this fake money is causing big trouble for everyone. It's been horrible in the east of Africa lately, and it's spreading like wildfire."

Aya couldn't hold back anymore. "But Grandma, where's all this fake cash coming from? Who's making it?"

Grandma looked up at Aya. "Now that," she said with a twinkle in her eye, "is the million-dollar question. Even the spirits might have trouble with that one! But we've got clues, and where there are clues, there's always a way to solve the mystery. Let's see what else your dad can tell us."

She went back to studying the shells, gently moving them around like she was solving a puzzle. Boubou and Aya waited, their hearts pounding with excitement, ready to crack this case wide open.

Grandma squinted hard at the cowrie shells, like she was trying to read the tiniest writing ever. "Your dad's spirit is showing me something big," she said quietly. "Somewhere out there, there's a whole bunch of expert counterfeiters. They're so good at making fake money that most people can't even tell the difference. It's got all the important people in a real tizzy."

Boubou held up their fake bill to the light. "So this is one of theirs?"

"Looks like it," Grandma nodded, eyeing the bill. "They've been making tons of tens and twenties. But that guy you met? He's probably just a small part of it all, trying to swap as much fake money for real cash as he can. He probably thought kids would be easier to trick with a smaller bill. Or maybe he got tricked himself and was just trying to get rid of it."

Grandma looked tired as she slowly stood up. The trip and all this mystical stuff had worn her out. "I should start cooking dinner," she said, wiping her forehead.

Aya joked, "I wish that guy had tried to give us a fake hundred instead. At least we'd be fifty bucks richer!"

Grandma laughed, some of her tiredness disappearing. "Oh, sweetie, then we'd be in even bigger trouble! Let's be glad it wasn't worse." With that, she headed to the kitchen, moving slow but steady, ready to switch from solving mysteries to making dinner.

✳ ✳ ✳

CHAPTER THREE

Mischief At The Morning Bell

If Boubou and Aya thought their counterfeit mishap would stay secret, their first day back at Zinguichou Middle School proved them wrong. As soon as they hit the front steps, their friend Mouhamed (the class clown) came up with a giant grin and a hilariously bad drawing of a fifty-dollar bill.

"Hey guys," he said, trying not to laugh. "My great-grandma just died in Zakar, and I need train fare for the funeral. Can you break this fifty for me?"

Before he even finished, their classmates burst out laughing. Somehow, everyone knew about their goof-up! Boubou and Aya tried to smile, but Aya's face turned as red as a tomato.

Mouhamed kept up his act. "What's wrong? You can't make change? Really? You don't want to help me get to my poor great-grandma's funeral?" He pretended to wipe away a tear, making everyone crack up even more.

Boubou, trying to keep cool, said, "Sorry, Mouhamed, we're out of the money-changing business."

"Oh, retired already?" Mouhamed shot back. "After your big adventure yesterday?" More groans and giggles from the crowd.

Boubou and Aya shared a look. Sure, it was embarrassing, but at least their friends thought it was funny.

"Yep, we've officially hung up our money-changing hats," Aya said dryly, playing along.

Mouhamed gasped dramatically. "Oh no! I think this bill might be fake!" He stared at his silly drawing, then whipped out a huge magnifying glass. After a second of intense 'inspection', he looked up with a sad face. "It's definitely counterfeit. One of the best I've ever seen. If it wasn't for the typos 'In Flop We Trust' and our principal's face instead of George Washington's, I would've been totally fooled. Good thing you guys didn't fall for it. Nice job!" He shook their hands really hard, somehow keeping a straight face while everyone else cracked up.

Boubou and Aya couldn't help but laugh too. It was pretty funny when you thought about it. As they all headed into school, Aya whispered to Boubou, "Well, at least we're famous now!"

Boubou grinned. "Yeah, but next time, let's be famous for solving a case, not messing one up!"

The story of the fake fifty bucks had spread faster than gossip at a sleepover. It all started when Mr. Moumba chatted with Amath's mom, who told Amath, one of Boubou and Aya's best friends. Before you could say "counterfeit," Amath had spilled the beans to Adama and the rest of their crew.

Bacary, their friend with the awesome afro, couldn't resist teasing them. "You know, if you keep playing banker for every stranger who asks, you'll end up broke!" He was talking about the money Boubou and Aya had earned from cracking the Lighthouse case and busting that diamond smuggling ring.

Boubou grinned. "Don't worry, we've still got some cash stashed away. We've even saved up enough to buy a motorboat!"

Adama's eyes lit up like fireworks. "A motorboat? You guys are getting another boat?" Just like that, everyone forgot about the fake money and started buzzing about this new adventure.

Adama's question brought back memories of their last big case. It had been like something out of an action movie! Boubou and Aya had helped take down the Scorpion gang, a bunch of nasty smugglers who'd been causing trouble all over Zinguichor. The whole thing came to a crazy end on Pierre's dad's boat.

Picture this: Task force officers, led by a super-tough Sergeant, teamed up with Pierre and the Diouf siblings. There was gunfire, boats zooming around, and more excitement than a theme park ride! But it was Boubou who saved the day. He realized the only way to stop the bad guys from escaping was to blow up their boat. So, in a move that was equal parts genius and crazy, he used the gas tank on Pierre's dad's boat as a makeshift bomb!

BOOM! The explosion was like the grand finale of the best fireworks show ever. It sank the smugglers' boat and got them all caught.

As Boubou finished telling the story, his friends sat in awe. Bacary whistled. "Man, and I thought my summer was exciting because I learned to do a backflip!"

Aya laughed. "Yeah, it was pretty wild. But let's hope our next case doesn't involve blowing anything up. I think we've had enough explosions to last a lifetime!"

"So," Adama said, leaning in, "about this new motorboat…"

Boubou nodded at Adama's question. "Yep, we're getting our own boat. After what happened with Pierre's dad's boat during that crazy mission, we figured it's smart to have one we can use whenever."

Aya added with a grin, "So we won't feel so bad if we need to, you know, accidentally blow it up again."

Their friends' eyes went wide. Bouma, whose boxing prowess was well-known in school, said excitedly, "I call dibs on being one of the first passengers!"

"We're thinking about getting one like the one we got for Pierre," Aya explained.

Pierre, whose dad was a big deal in the local construction business, looked a little jealous. "I wish the new one was mine," he sighed, "but after I accidentally turned Dad's boat into fireworks last time, he won't even let me near a rubber ducky in the bathtub." He grinned sheepishly. "But hey, if you're getting a boat, go for something even cooler! Maybe one that's explosion-proof… you know, just in case."

Boubou shared what Grandma Diouf had told them. "She said we could get one as long as we stick to the bay or the Casamance River. She's worried we might try something crazy like sailing across the Atlantic!"

Djily, the football captain and the group's voice of reason, was not in a joking mood. "I guess our summer soccer league is toast now that you'll have this sweet new ride."

"Why?" Boubou asked, confused.

"If you get that boat," Djily said, shaking his head, "we'll never see you guys! You're already off exploring on your bikes half the time, and now you want to add boating to the mix?" He ran a hand through his hair, frustration clear on his face. "I've worked my butt off setting up this summer league. Losing our star striker and our ace goalie? That's like… like losing both arms before a boxing match!"

Boubou shrugged, a hint of a smile on his face. "Sorry, Djily, but a day out on the water or biking beats kicking a ball around any day."

Djily's eyes widened in disbelief. "Are you serious right now? Can't you at least show up for a few games? For the team?"

"Chill out," Boubou said, holding up his hands. "We'll be there for the games, promise. We're just not spending every free second practicing. There's a whole world out there to explore, you know?"

Aya nodded, adding, "Yeah, who knows? Maybe all this boating will improve our footwork. You ever tried to balance on a moving boat?"

Djily sighed, resigned. "I guess some games are better than no games."

Mouhamed, ever the jokester, piped up, "Just stay away from Kambossa's cliff this time. We don't need your new boat becoming a submarine!"

Amath, not one to miss out on a prank, decided it was Djily's turn for some teasing. "Hey Djily," he called out with a mischievous glint in his eye, "bet you can't even catch an easy pass these days." He exchanged a sly wink with Mouhamed, their silent signal for mischief.

Before Djily could protest, Amath whipped out a soccer ball from his backpack. He tossed it gently into the air, making it look like the easiest catch in the world.

"Seriously?" Djily scoffed, his pride a little wounded. "Watch and learn, amateurs."

As Djily stepped forward to make the catch, Mouhamed silently dropped to his hands and knees right behind him. Meanwhile, Amath's "easy" toss suddenly gained some spin, forcing Djily to step back.

It happened in a split second. Djily, focused on the ball, didn't see Mouhamed. His heel caught on Mouhamed's back, and suddenly, Djily was flailing like a cartoon character. With a surprised yelp, he toppled over, landing in an ungraceful heap as the ball bounced mockingly beside him.

The schoolyard erupted in laughter. Djily scrambled to his feet, his face mixed with embarrassment and playful anger. "You sneaks!" he yelled, charging after a cackling Mouhamed, who was already sprinting away.

Amath scooped up the ball, grinning triumphantly. "See? Told you he couldn't catch it," he declared, puffing out his chest in mock superiority.

Just as the laughter reached its peak, the school bell rang out, loud and insistent. It was like someone had flipped a switch, turning their playground antics into a mad dash for class. Still chuckling, the friends gathered their bags, their morning fun giving way to the school day ahead.

❖

Boubou, Aya, and their friends joined the stampede of students squeezing through the school's front doors. The hallway was a zoo of noise—lockers clanging, sneakers squeaking, and a hundred conversations all at once. It was like someone had flipped a switch, turning their goofy playground antics into serious school mode.

As they weaved through the crowd, Boubou caught Aya's eye. They shared a final grin, both thinking about their crazy morning—fake money, boat dreams, and Djily's epic wipeout. Who knew what the rest of the day would bring?

With quick fist bumps and "see ya laters," the group split up, each heading to their own classroom. But even as they settled into their desks and pulled out their books, a spark of excitement lingered. Sure, they had to focus on fractions and geography for now, but afterward? Well, that's when the real adventures would begin!

CHAPTER FOUR

From Fifty To Five Hundred

As Boubou Diouf settled into his seat that sunny morning, his eyes wandered two rows over to Aminata Correa's desk. Aminata, with her flowing hair and sparkling eyes, was easily one of the prettiest girls at Zinguichou High. To Boubou, she outshone all the other girls in town. Every day, he'd look her way, and she'd flash a smile so bright it made the dusty classroom feel magical. On days she was absent, everything felt off, like a soccer game without a ball. The whole day just didn't make sense without her smile lighting up the classroom.

But today was different. Aminata was there, but her usual sparkle was gone. She was buried in her books, completely missing Boubou's hopeful glance. Without her smile, Boubou sat there, mouth hanging open like a fish out of water, before awkwardly turning back to his own books. His mind was a jumble all morning. What could he have done to upset Aminata? The thought bugged him like an itch he couldn't scratch.

He replayed yesterday's events in his head. Maybe she'd heard about him being tricked by that stranger and thought he was a dummy. But no, that didn't sound like Aminata. She wasn't the type to judge without good reason. He tried to shake it off but couldn't help sneaking peeks at her all morning, hoping for a clue.

Their silent morning hello had always been their special thing, a secret moment just for them in the middle of boring school stuff. For Boubou, it was the highlight of his day, a tiny thread connecting him to Aminata. Today, that thread felt broken, and it left him feeling lost.

Aminata was so unlike herself. She barely looked up from her books, and when the teacher called on her, her answers were distracted and distant. Something was clearly eating at her, something way bigger than normal school drama.

When recess came, Aminata's mood became even more obvious. She drifted out of class alone, looking like a gray cloud in a sea of colorful umbrellas. Boubou watched as she found a quiet spot on the grass, staring at a soccer game but turning down invitations to play.

Determined to figure out what was wrong, Boubou plopped down next to her on the grass. "What's up, Aminata?" he asked, worry evident in his voice.

Aminata looked up, her smile weak but there. "Oh, hey Boubou. Fancy meeting you here," she said, a tiny spark of her usual humor peeking through.

"I've been right across from you all morning, you know," Boubou teased gently. "It's like I turned invisible or something."

"Sorry, Boubou. I know I'm not myself today. Just got a lot on my mind," Aminata admitted, her eyes showing how upset she was.

"Something wrong?" Boubou prodded carefully.

She nodded, her face getting serious. "It's about money."

Boubou's forehead wrinkled in confusion. Aminata lived with her cousin, Miss Nala Correa, a well-known beautician in the city. They weren't rich, but Miss Correa made enough for them to live comfortably. Plus, Aminata's parents, who lived in the countryside, regularly sent money for her school stuff. Boubou couldn't figure out why money would be a problem for her.

Puzzled, he asked, "Is there an issue with your allowance? Did it not come through this time?"

"No, it's not about my allowance," Aminata began, worry clear in her voice. "It's about Nala. She lost a bunch of money. Way more than we can just shrug off."

"Lost money? How'd that happen?" Boubou leaned in, sensing this was serious.

Aminata took a deep breath, "She lost five hundred dollars last night."

Boubou let out a low whistle, "Whoa, that's no small change."

"It really isn't," Aminata's voice was heavy with worry. "What makes it worse is that Nala had just finished paying for new stuff for her beauty shop – fancy lights, mirrors, all that jazz. It left her pretty tight on cash. It's hard seeing her so stressed."

Boubou leaned closer, "But how did she lose it?"

Aminata explained, "A customer came in last night and bought a bunch of beauty products, about 120 bucks worth. She paid with a 500-dollar bill. The register was full 'cause it was the end of the day, and Nala, not wanting to lose the sale, gave her the change."

Boubou's face turned serious; he had a feeling he knew where this was going. "And the bill was fake," he said, not really asking.

Aminata looked at him, surprised. "How'd you know it was fake?"

Boubou hesitated, then sighed. "Actually, I had my own run-in with counterfeit money recently. A stranger at the station tricked me and Aya with a fake bill."

"What?" Aminata's eyes widened. "You never mentioned that!"

"Yeah, it just happened yesterday," Boubou explained. "We're actually looking into it now. Seems like there's a bunch of fake money going around Zinguichou."

Aminata shook her head in disbelief. "First fifty bucks, now five hundred. This is bigger than I thought."

"It really is," Boubou agreed, his face serious. "I feel awful for Nala, losing that much."

"Yeah, it's a real punch in the gut," Aminata sighed. "She'll be okay, but losing money like that is never easy. Especially that much."

Still processing the story, Boubou asked, "Did Nala recognize the woman who gave her the bill?"

Aminata shook her head. "Total stranger. Super fancy and good-looking, so Nala didn't suspect a thing. It wasn't until later, when Nala read about fake money warnings in the newspaper that she started to worry."

"That's just like what happened to me with the fifty," Boubou noted, seeing the similarities.

Aminata nodded, "Yeah, Nala called Mr. Sousou from the bank. He checked the bill and said it was definitely fake. But he also admitted it was a pretty good copy."

Boubou's face turned serious. "Did Nala tell the police?"

"I think she already did," Aminata replied, sounding a bit frustrated. "But honestly, she's not getting her hopes up. You know how the police are around here – they're not exactly known for solving these kinds of cases quickly. Most of the time, they just end up in a big pile of unsolved mysteries. So she gave me the bill to pass on to you."

"Really? That's awesome," Boubou's eyes lit up with excitement and determination. "Aya and I are actually looking into this fake money business. Do you have the bill with you?"

"It's in my bag in the cloakroom. I'll grab it for you at lunch," Aminata promised.

Boubou nodded, his mind buzzing with excitement. This was a huge break in their case! He could already picture himself and Aya cracking the mystery wide open. But what really made his heart do a little dance was the idea of helping Aminata.

"Don't worry, Aminata," he said, puffing up his chest just a tiny bit. "Aya and I are on this case, and now we've got an even bigger clue. We'll get to the bottom of this fake money business."

Aminata's eyes lit up with hope. "Really? You think you can figure it out?"

"We'll sure try our best," Boubou grinned, feeling like a superhero in the making. "It's not just about solving a cool mystery anymore. It's about protecting our town, our friends... and your family's business too."

He felt a warm glow of pride as Aminata smiled gratefully at him. This wasn't just about impressing her anymore - though that was definitely a bonus. It was about doing something real, something important. Boubou straightened up, feeling the weight of responsibility on his shoulders. He and Aya had a job to do, and now, more than ever, he was determined to succeed.

❖

As the final bell rang, signaling the end of classes and the start of lunch break, Aminata hurried over to Boubou, a crisp bill clutched in her hand. Her eyes were a swirl of worry and hope as she passed it to him.

Boubou took the fake $500 note and studied it closely. It looked brand new, just like the $50 bill he and Aya had fallen for yesterday. While Boubou hadn't seen many $500 bills in his life - real or fake - he had to admit this one was pretty convincing. He wondered if the fact that such big bills were rare actually made them easier to sneak past people.

"I'll get this to Aya right away," Boubou promised, trying to sound confident for Aminata's sake. "We can't work miracles, but we'll do our best. Nala might have to write off the loss unless we find the woman who passed this bill. But maybe, just maybe, this could lead us to whoever's making these fakes."

Aminata's face was a mix of emotions. "It's awful to think how many people are getting tricked by these phonies, just like Nala," she said softly. "I really hope you and Aya can help catch the creeps behind all this."

Boubou felt a surge of determination. Seeing Aminata so worried made him want to solve this case more than ever. He puffed up his chest a little, trying to look reassuring. "We'll crack this mystery wide open, you'll see. Nobody messes with our town and gets away with it!"

As Aya plopped down next to Boubou on the school steps, he couldn't wait to spill the beans about Nala Correa's beauty parlor disaster.

"Get this," Boubou started, his eyes wide with excitement, "Nala got totally bamboozled out of five hundred bucks by some slick customer!"

"No way!" Aya gasped. "How'd that happen?"

"Well," Boubou leaned in, lowering his voice, "she might not have known the bill was fake at first. But here's the thing - I'm starting to think this is way bigger than we thought. There could be a whole gang of them, cruising around, spreading these bogus bills like confetti."

Aya's forehead wrinkled in thought as Boubou continued, "Once these fake bills are out there, they just keep bouncing from person to person until some bank catches on. And you know who always loses out? The good guys. They're the ones who figure out the money's fake and stop using it. The bad guys? They just keep passing those phony bills as fast as they can."

"That's messed up," Aya shook her head. "So what do we do now?"

Boubou grinned, a spark of determination in his eye. "Now? We put on our detective hats and follow the money trail. These counterfeiters picked the wrong town to mess with!"

As soon as they burst through the front door, Boubou couldn't wait to fill Grandma Diouf in on Nala Correa's money mishap. He handed over the suspicious bill like it was a hot potato.

"Good grief, they're pushing big bills now?" Grandma Diouf's eyes went wide as she studied the note.

"Do you think it's the same bunch that tricked us with that fake fifty?" Aya piped up, practically buzzing with curiosity.

Boubou, feeling every bit the detective, dug out a magnifying glass from his dad's old desk. He started examining the bill like it was a rare butterfly. "It's tricky to say for sure," he muttered, his nose practically touching the paper. "These fakes are so good, you'd need a real pro to spot the differences."

He grabbed the fifty-dollar bill they'd been duped with earlier and compared them side by side, squinting through the magnifying glass. After what felt like forever, he finally pocketed the glass with a satisfied nod.

"I'd bet my lunch money they came from the same place," Boubou declared, sounding more like a TV detective than a kid. "The paper feels almost the same, just a tiny bit lighter than real money. And there are these itty-bitty details in the picture part that look super similar on both bills."

"Aminata won't mind if we hang onto this for our investigation, right?" Grandma Diouf asked, her voice a mix of worry and intrigue.

Boubou grinned, "Are you kidding? She'll be thrilled we're on the case!"

Aya nodded confidently. "She's way more interested in catching the bad guys, so keeping it is no big deal. It's not like it's worth anything real anyway," she pointed out.

Grandma Diouf's face fell as she thought about Aminata's tough situation. "It's just awful, really. To think there are folks out there making fake money, knowing full well it's the everyday people who'll end up hurting. It's shameful," she sighed.

"You got that right, Grandma," Boubou agreed, his voice serious. "Some people will do anything for a quick buck. But once we get the expert's opinion on these bills, we might have a real clue to follow."

Boubou's face lit up with an idea. "We should send these bills to a pro in the city. Dad had this friend, a real expert on this stuff. He helped Dad out loads of times."

Aya's eyes sparked with determination. "And if we find out it's one big gang behind all this, we'll need to be super careful. Everyone in town will have to keep their eyes peeled for anything fishy."

"We're gonna crack this mystery wide open; just you wait and see!" Boubou said.

* * *

CHAPTER FIVE

The Last Laugh

THE WEEK ZOOMED BY IN A WHIRLWIND OF FRANTIC studying. Boubou, Aya, and their classmates were drowning in a sea of textbooks as exam week inched closer. Even Djily, who usually cared more about scoring goals than acing tests, was scrambling to finish his mountain of homework. Boubou and Aya hunched over their history books, groaning about the endless parade of ancient heroes and empire builders they had to memorize.

"Why do we have to learn about a bunch of dusty old dudes who lived a gazillion years ago?" Aya huffed, dramatically flopping onto her desk. "I bet none of them ever had to suffer through exams!"

Boubou nodded in agreement. "Yeah, they were too busy conquering stuff to worry about pop quizzes. Must've been nice."

As they scribbled notes about long-gone civilizations, both friends couldn't help daydreaming about the sunny playground just outside their classroom window. The cheerful shouts of younger kids enjoying recess floated through the air, making their textbooks seem even more boring by comparison.

❖

Finally, Friday night rolled around, marking the end of their brain-melting week of grammar drills, math problems, and historical dates. Eager to leave the school blues far behind, they huddled up to plan their weekend escape.

As they burst out of school on Friday, Boubou bounced with excitement. "Let's ditch the city tomorrow and head out to the countryside!"

Adama nodded eagerly. "Yeah! And let's hoof it - no bikes or anything. Just good old-fashioned walking power."

Djily, still football-obsessed, couldn't help himself. "Or… we could hit the field for some practice?"

Bouma playfully squared up, fists raised. "Mention football one more time, and you'll get a taste of my famous noogie attack! School's the last thing we want to think about until Monday, and even that's too soon."

"Whoa, easy there, tiger," Djily backpedaled, hands up in surrender. "Just throwing it out there, you know?"

"And I'm just saying, let's put that idea on ice," Amath chimed in. He dug into his Mary Poppins-like pockets and fished out a peanut. "Here, munch on this and chill out."

Djily, always up for a snack, happily snagged the peanut. "So, where are we heading on this nature adventure?" he asked, the peanut shell cracking between his teeth.

"How about Salimata Toure's farm?" Aya suggested. "Grandma's been yakking about making mango jam. She's hoping Toure might let her snag some mangoes this year. We could ask while we're there."

"Sounds like a plan to me," Djily agreed, chomping down.

Suddenly, his eyes bulged like a cartoon character. His face twisted in shock, then panic. Tears sprang to his eyes as his jaw clamped shut. He let out a strangled squeak and spat out the peanut, then started hopping around the sidewalk like he was on a pogo stick, arms flailing wildly.

Amath watched with mock seriousness. "Ooh, looks like he's doing the Spicy Chicken Dance!" He started clapping along. "Bravo, Djily! Encore!"

"Fire!" Djily wheezed. "My mouth is on fire! Need... water!"

"Quick, someone call the fire department!" Amath said between fits of laughter.

The gang watched Djily's unexpected performance, eyes wide as saucers. But as he kept flailing and choking, they couldn't help but burst into giggles. Desperate for relief, Djily spun around, making a beeline for the school's water fountain.

As they watched Djily's frantic water quest, Boubou and Aya hung back, torn between worry and amusement. Aya leaned in, whispering, "Does Amath ever take a day off from Prankster Duty?"

Boubou, eyes glued to Djily's water-seeking mission, replied, "Nah, I think he's gunning for the World Prank Champion title."

"You think maybe he does all this for attention?" Aya wondered aloud, still watching the chaos unfold.

Djily, blinded by chili-induced tears, missed the flower bed's wire border and face-planted right into a bunch of petunias.

Boubou winced. "Well, he's definitely in the spotlight now."

Aya nodded, stifling a giggle. "Total class clown. It's like every prank is shouting, 'Look at me!'"

Banene, the grumpy school janitor, had been watching the whole thing with a rare smile. But when Djily crashed into his prized flower bed, that smile vanished faster than cookies at a bake sale. "Get outta there!" he bellowed, his accent thicker than peanut butter. "Scram, you little troublemaker! I'm gonna report you!"

"Amath means well, though," Boubou added quickly. "His pranks are just for laughs, never mean."

"True," Aya agreed, still watching the show. "I guess it's his way of spicing things up around here."

The others scattered like spooked cats. Djily, still desperate for water, scrambled up, barely escaping Banene's grasp. In the chaos,

Banene himself tripped over the wire, crushing flowers and getting tangled up.

Boubou grinned. "Well, Amath's definitely got a flair for drama. Poor Djily, though. Always the unlucky target."

"I guess that's what makes our crew so interesting," Aya smirked. "You never know what Amath's cooking up next."

Djily finally reached the fountain, gulping water like a camel at an oasis. Banene, now spouting words that definitely weren't in any schoolbooks, freed himself and charged at Djily. With one last longing look at the fountain and a panicked glance at the incoming janitor-shaped missile, Djily knew it was time to vamoose.

"Keeps us on our toes, for sure," Boubou chuckled. "I just hope I'm not next on his prank hit list!"

"With Amath around, anything's possible," Aya replied, eyes twinkling. "But that's part of the fun, right?"

Djily rejoined his friends at the street corner, still chuckling and admitting he'd fallen for the joke hook, line, and sinker. Meanwhile, Banene gave up the chase, grumbling about Monday payback.

"Chill out, he'll forget all about it by Monday," Adama said confidently.

"He might, but I won't," Djily said, a mischievous glint in his eye. "Next time someone offers me a peanut, I'm asking for an apple. Can't hide chili in that! Watch your back, Amath. Payback's coming."

"Bring it on, Spicy Dancer," Amath shot back with a grin.

"Alright, prank wars later," Adama cut in. "Let's get back to planning our great escape tomorrow!"

The sun was barely peeking over the horizon when the Diouf siblings and their friends gathered in the old barn behind Adama's house. They were all geared up for their big hike, looking like a bunch of mini explorers ready to conquer the world. Not everyone could make it - some were stuck with chores or buried under mountains of homework. But those who did show up came armed with lunches that could feed an army, courtesy of their moms who knew that adventuring on an empty stomach was a recipe for disaster.

Amath and Djily were running fashionably late, as usual. This allowed the others to warm up in the barn, which they'd turned into a makeshift gym over the years.

Bouma was unleashing a fury of punches on the bag, his left hooks and uppercuts making it buzz like an angry beehive. "Take that!" he grunted, imagining he was fending off a pack of wild animals. The bag swung wildly with each hit, barely surviving Bouma's relentless assault.

"Whoa there, champ!" Adama called out, momentarily distracted from his lunch dilemma. "Leave some energy for the hike!"

Bouma paused, wiping sweat from his brow. "Just warming up," he panted with a grin. "Gotta be ready for anything out there in the wild!"

Meanwhile, Boubou was attempting some ninja moves on the climbing bars. He twisted and turned like a pretzel, practicing for future tree-climbing escapades. "Watch this!" he called out, before nearly losing his grip and ending up as a Boubou pancake on the barn floor.

Adama, on the other hand, was having an intense staring contest with his lunchbox. His stomach grumbled as he debated whether it was too early to sneak a bite of his mom's famous chocolate cake. "Maybe just a tiny slice," he muttered, his hand inching towards the box.

Just as Adama was about to commit the ultimate pre-hike crime, Amath burst through the door, a bandana making him look like a pint-sized pirate. Djily stumbled in behind him, still yawning.

"Avast, ye lazy landlubbers!" Amath bellowed in his best (worst) pirate voice. "Are ye ready for adventure?"

With the gang finally assembled, they set off into the great unknown (also known as the countryside just outside town). They marched along, whistling off-key and chattering excitedly, ready for whatever the day might throw at them.

"Last one to the big oak tree is a rotten egg!" Boubou yelled suddenly, breaking into a run.

The others quickly gave chase, their laughter echoing in the crisp morning air. Another Diouf adventure was officially underway!

❖

They kept it cool while still in town, but once they hit the dusty country roads, all bets were off. They playfully shoved each other, raced like wild horses, and snagged berries from bushes along the way. Their laughter bounced off the hills, free as birds in the open air.

The gang followed the winding Cazamoun River, zigzagging through farms and rolling hills near Zabrousse. When the sun climbed high, they veered off the road, diving under the shade of trees toward a secret swimming hole. They splashed and swam like a bunch of happy otters for what felt like forever.

Amath, the group's resident trickster, was first to dry off. With an evil glint in his eye, he set about turning everyone's clothes into the world's most complicated knots. When the others discovered his handiwork, they scrambled out of the water like startled cats, chasing Amath into a nearby thicket. But their revenge was short-lived - the thorns were like tiny daggers on their bare feet, sending them hopping back to the riverbank.

"How's that t-shirt pretzel treating you?" Amath called out, barely containing his giggles.

"Just you wait!" Aya grumbled, gnawing at a particularly stubborn knot with her teeth.

"I'll be right here," Amath sang back, his voice dripping with mischief.

"You're so dead," Djily muttered under his breath.

"And you won't even see it coming," Boubou added with a sly grin.

Once they finally wrestled free from their tangled clothes, the gang took off after Amath like a pack of hungry wolves. Despite his head start, Amath's legs soon turned to jelly, and they caught him right at the entrance to Salimata Toure's farm. In a flurry of giggles and shouts, they stripped him of his shoes, lunch, and lucky bandana.

"Time for a taste of your own medicine, prankster!" Boubou declared. He chucked one of Amath's shoes into a field where a grumpy-looking bull was munching grass, and sent the other flying into a patch of prickly thistles.

Djily, still steaming, wrapped Amath's bandana around his neck in a knot that would make a sailor proud. "Have fun solving this puzzle, buddy," he smirked.

"And enjoy your invisible lunch," Adama added, dangling Amath's food from a tree branch down the road.

Bouma and Djily finally released Amath, who they'd been pinning down in the middle of the lane. "Catch you at the farm… if you make it!" Bouma called over his shoulder as they all headed towards Toure's place, still giggling like hyenas.

Amath, muttering empty threats, set off on his quest to reclaim his stuff. First up: grabbing his shoe from the bull's field. He approached the fence, eyeing the massive animal warily.

"Okay, Mr. Bull," he whispered, "let's be friends. I just need my shoe, and I'll be out of your hair… uh, fur."

Amath hopped the fence with all the grace of a sack of potatoes. The bull's head snapped up, a look of bovine disbelief in its eyes.

"Nice bull," Amath cooed, inching towards his shoe. "Good bull. You don't want to play with a smelly old shoe, do you?"

The bull disagreed. With a snort that sounded suspiciously like laughter, it pawed the ground and charged.

Amath yelped and ran in zigzags, feeling like the world's slowest matador. He dove for his shoe, grabbed it, and sprinted for the fence. But the bull was faster.

In a moment of panic-induced genius, Amath hurled his newly-recovered shoe at the bull's face. It bounced off the animal's nose with a comical 'honk,' momentarily confusing it.

Seizing his chance, Amath scrambled up the fence. But his victory was short-lived. His pants caught on a nail, leaving him dangling upside down on the wrong side of the fence, face-to-face with a very unamused bull.

"Nice... bull?" Amath squeaked.

The bull's response was to headbutt the fence, sending Amath flying into a conveniently placed mud puddle on the other side. He emerged, sputtering and covered in muck, to find his shoe had somehow landed perfectly on his head.

"Well," he muttered, plucking the shoe from his new mud-helmet, "at least I got what I came for."

As he squelched away, he could've sworn he heard bovine laughter behind him.

But Amath's misery was far from over. His next challenge: retrieving his other shoe from the dreaded Thistle Zone. He stood at the edge, eyeing the prickly minefield with the wariness of a cartoon character about to step on a rake.

"Okay, Amath," he pep-talked himself, "it's just a bunch of plants. How bad can it be?"

He took one ginger step into the patch and immediately regretted his life choices. "Yeow!" he yelped, hopping from one foot to the other like he was dancing on hot coals.

Determined, Amath tried a new strategy. He got down on all fours, attempting to crawl through the thistles. This worked great... for about three seconds. Then he yelped again as his hands and knees discovered that thistles were, in fact, quite prickly.

In a flash of inspiration (or maybe desperation), Amath grabbed a large piece of tree bark. "I'll surf through!" he declared triumphantly. He tossed the bark onto the thistles and leaped onto it.

For a glorious moment, he felt like a genius. Then physics remembered it had a job to do. The bark tipped, catapulting Amath face-first into the thickest patch of thistles yet.

He emerged looking like a very grumpy porcupine, his hair full of prickly souvenirs. But there, just within reach, was his shoe!

With a victorious cry that sounded more like a whimper, Amath snatched his prize. He limped out of the Thistle Zone, plucking prickles from places he didn't even know could be prickled.

"Next time," he grumbled, inspecting a particularly impressive thistle stuck to his nose, "I'm just going barefoot."

❖

The last they saw of him, Amath was perched on a rock by the road, yanking thistles from his feet, hands, and face and staring at the tangled mess around his neck like an alien puzzle.

"Bet he's learned his lesson now," Aya said with a snort as they reached Toure's farm.

"Don't count on it," Boubou replied, shaking his head. "I bet his brain's already cooking up his next prank."

* * *

CHAPTER SIX

Mysteries At The Power Plant

MR. TOURE, TALL AND LANKY WITH A NATURAL SLOUCH, shuffled in from the fields just as Boubou and Aya swung open the barnyard gate. His mustache drooped like his shoulders, and dangling from his lips was his ever-present, slightly droopy pipe.

The old farmer had a quirky talent that never failed to amaze: he could chew on his toothpick and puff on his pipe at the same time. It was like watching a magician, except Mr. Toure's magic trick involved juggling the toothpick and pipe, pausing only for a quick swap or refill. It was a local legend; some folks claimed they'd seen him without the toothpick, others without the pipe, but nobody could say they'd ever seen Mr. Toure without at least one of them in his mouth.

Adama, known for his tall tales, once swore up and down that Mr. Toure slept with the pipe clenched between his teeth and a stash of toothpicks within reach, switching between them even in his dreams.

"Hey there, kiddos!" Mr. Toure greeted them, clamping the pipe more firmly between his lips. "What's the scoop? What brings you to my neck of the woods?"

Aya wrinkled her nose slightly. "Mr. Toure, you know smoking's bad for you, right? We learned all about it in health class last week."

Mr. Toure chuckled, the pipe wobbling precariously. "Ah, you young'uns and your modern ideas. This pipe's been with me longer than you've been alive!"

"But Aya's right," Boubou chimed in. "It can make you really sick. Plus, it makes your breath smell like Grandpa's old shoes."

Mr. Toure raised an eyebrow, amused. "Is that so? Well, I appreciate your concern, but this old dog's not learning any new tricks. Now, what can I do for you two today?"

Knowing they were not going to change his mind, Boubou changed the subject: "How's the mango crop looking this year, Mr. Toure?"

Mr. Toure grunted noncommittally. "Eh, it's okay, I guess. Fair to middling, maybe."

Getting a positive word out of Mr. Toure was as rare as snow in July. If he said the crops were poor, they were probably not too bad. And if he said they were "fair to middling," well, that was practically a rave review.

"Our grandma was wondering," Boubou continued, "if you'd be willing to share some mangos for canning this year?"

Chomping thoughtfully on his toothpick, Mr. Toure seemed to ponder the request, his pipe momentarily forgotten.

"Sure thing, she can count on it," Mr. Toure nodded. "Tell Grandma Diouf to expect a bumper crop of mangos come harvest time. I've always got plenty for her."

"Awesome, thanks, Mr. Toure! That was actually the main reason we stopped by," Boubou said with a grateful smile.

Mr. Toure, now more relaxed, leaned against the fence, his hands buried deep in the pockets of his weathered overalls. As he eyed the siblings, the toothpick danced a little jig under his mustache.

"Out for a bit of an adventure, are you?" he asked casually.

"Yep, it seemed like the perfect day to explore," Aya replied, her eyes scanning the horizon.

Mr. Toure nodded, squinting up at the sky as if double-checking the weather. "Nice day for a wander, alright. Any particular destination in mind?"

"We're just roaming around, seeing where the day takes us," Boubou shrugged.

Mr. Toure's eyes narrowed slightly. "You're not planning on heading towards the old power plant, down that abandoned road by the river, are you?"

Aya perked up. "The old power plant? We hadn't really thought about it. Why? Is there something we should know?"

The toothpick's dance grew more vigorous, mirroring Mr. Toure's growing concern. He took a thoughtful puff from his pipe, which was threatening to go out. "Well, it's just... I'd steer clear if I were you," he finally said, exhaling a cloud of smoke.

"But why?" Boubou pressed. "Sure, it's run-down and all, but we can be careful."

Mr. Toure shifted uncomfortably. "It's not about being careful. The place isn't empty anymore."

Aya and Boubou exchanged a puzzled look. "What do you mean, Mr. Toure? Who's there?" Aya asked.

"Three guys have taken over the old power plant," Mr. Toure explained. "Weird bunch, if you ask me. Set up shop there a few weeks back."

The news visibly surprised the siblings. The town's old hydroelectric power plant, nestled along a wild stretch of the Cazamoun River, had once buzzed with activity. But when the demand for electricity in the growing city and nearby villages outgrew the small plant's capacity, newer, bigger power plants had turned it into a ghostly relic, its wheel silent for years. The thought of it springing back to life was unexpected, to say the least.

"Maybe they're turning it into a millet power plant, then?" Boubou asked jokingly, trying to make sense of it.

"Nope," Mr. Toure said, shaking his head. "But their whole operation... let's just say it's fishier than last week's catch. I dared to ask about it once, and they nearly whacked me with a stick. I'll stick with the power plant in Zinguichou, thank you very much."

"So, like, what's their plan for business in this area?" Aya wondered aloud.

"They're not really looking to work with local farmers, as far as I can tell," Mr. Toure mused, scratching his chin. "They said something about developing a new type of super-battery, some kind of tech breakthrough. And they're keeping it hush-hush, waiting on patents and all that jazz. They're so secretive, they won't even let anyone peek inside the power plant."

"Three men, and they're all… kind of unfriendly?" Boubou asked, trying to picture them.

"Yeah, three of them. Not exactly winning any congeniality contests. Oh, and there's a kid with them, almost forgot. A young one, about your age," he said, pointing at Aya. "Never seen any of them before. My guess? They're city slickers, looking for a quiet place to work on their mysterious battery invention. That's why I'm saying you kids might want to steer clear. They don't seem to take kindly to nosy neighbors."

Djily's eyes lit up with a spark of adventure. "Now I really want to see this place," he declared.

The rest of the group murmured in agreement, their curiosity piqued by the unfolding mystery.

Mr. Toure, with a casual shrug, gave his tacit approval. "Well, it's your call. Just remember, I told you they're not exactly the welcoming committee. But it's none of my business, really."

"We'll be careful not to bug them," Boubou reassured him, already excited about the prospect. "What do you guys think? Should we head over there?"

The allure of a good mystery was like a magnet to the group. The idea of the old hydroelectric power plant humming back to life, shrouded in secrecy, was too tempting to resist.

"Let's take the abandoned road and check it out," Aya proposed, her adventurous spirit taking over. "It's a destination, at least."

Adama, always ready for a bit of excitement, chimed in, "We can have our lunch on the way. It'll be an adventure."

Boubou, with a grin, summed up the group's sentiment. "Looks like we're all in agreement. Off to the power plant it is!"

Mr. Toure, still chewing on his toothpick, couldn't help but smile slyly. "Just remember, if you end up being chased off, don't say I didn't warn you." His eyes twinkled with mischief. Unbeknownst to the kids, he was partly driven by his own curiosity about the newcomers at the abandoned power plant. Maybe, just maybe, the siblings could uncover some details he hadn't been able to.

"Enjoy your hike," Mr. Toure said, returning to his farmhouse. "And try not to find too much trouble."

"We'll be fine," they called back, already embarking on their path down the lane, eager to uncover the secrets of the old power plant.

As they continued their journey, they ran into Amath, who was trudging along, kicking up a cloud of dust. He'd managed to gather up his scattered stuff after their earlier prank. Far from being mad, Amath seemed to be in a great mood, a big grin spreading across his face as he spotted his friends.

"Feeling pretty smug, huh?" he teased, his voice playful as they got closer. "My feet have so many thistles, you guys totally owe me a piggyback ride home."

Amath started to hobble with an over-the-top limp to make his point, acting like he was completely wiped out from his earlier scramble for socks and shoes.

Boubou laughed and said, "We wouldn't carry you even if it was just to the end of this lane! You better keep up if you want to join us."

Amath's eyes sparkled with curiosity. "Where's the big adventure today?"

"We're checking out the old power plant," Boubou replied. "Mr. Toure says it's back in business."

Amath's face lit up with excitement. "No way! Last one there's a rotten egg!" And with that, he took off like a rocket, his fake foot pain totally forgotten. He led the way, turning their walk into a wild race towards the old power plant road.

The group, caught up in the fun, chased after him. Aya, not to be outdone, yelled, "Hey, no fair! You got a head start!"

Puffing as he ran, Boubou added, "Yeah, what happened to those thistle-filled feet, huh?"

Amath just laughed, calling over his shoulder, "Miracle cure! Nothing like a good adventure to fix sore feet!"

Their laughter and playful trash talk filled the air as they raced towards their mysterious destination, the old power plant growing closer with every step.

CHAPTER SEVEN

A Splash Of Fate

THE SUN WAS HIGH IN THE SKY WHEN THE DIOUF SIBLINGS and their friends reached the old, abandoned power plant. They'd been hiking for about an hour and decided to take a lunch break under the shady trees lining the quiet road. After refueling with sandwiches and snacks, they climbed to the top of a hill that gave them a perfect view of the river below.

The power plant looked like something out of a spooky movie. Its giant wheel creaked and groaned as it turned slowly, almost as if it was complaining about being woken up after a long nap.

As they got closer to the entrance, they spotted three figures in the distance - two men and a boy. At first, they couldn't make out much, but as they crept down the hill, they could see the men more clearly. They were middle-aged and looked kind of scruffy, like they hadn't shaved or changed clothes in a while.

Remembering what old Mr. Toure had told them earlier about being careful, the kids used the overgrown bushes along the old road to hide. They snuck down so quietly that no one noticed them, and soon they were only about a hundred yards from the power plant, perfectly hidden in the leaves.

"I don't like the looks of those guys," Boubou whispered, his stomach doing a little flip.

"Me neither," Aya agreed, her eyes narrowing as she studied the men.

One of the men, probably in his fifties, had a scraggly grey beard and glasses perched on his nose. He wore overalls that had definitely seen better days, with the sleeves rolled up to show arms stained from hard work.

Boubou squinted, noticing something odd. "His hands are weirdly clean for a guy who's supposed to be working in a dusty old power plant. »

"He looks more like he's been polishing cars than messing with rusty machines," Aya added.

The other man seemed older and was dressed similarly, but he had a kinder look about him. He didn't wear glasses, but his bushy eyebrows were so thick they almost hid his sharp eyes. He stroked his long white beard as he listened to the other man talk in a low voice.

The Diouf siblings strained their ears but couldn't hear what the men were saying. Then they noticed a boy, about ten or eleven, with curly black hair and clothes that looked like they'd been through a paper shredder. He said something to the older man, whose friendly expression suddenly vanished. He smacked the boy's ear, making him stumble.

"Beat it!" the old man yelled, his voice easily reaching the kids' hiding places. Go play somewhere else. Don't hang around while we're talking."

But the boy stood his ground and repeated whatever he'd said before. This made the old man even angrier.

"I said go play!" he screeched, his face turning red. "I'll call you when I need you. And you better come running when I do!" He grabbed a heavy walking stick leaning by the door and swung it at the boy, who dodged it like a pro and took off running towards the back of the power plant. The old man glared after him, muttering words that would definitely get Boubou and Aya grounded if they repeated them.

"Leave the kid alone," the other man growled, his voice sounding like he'd gargled with gravel. "We've got more important things to worry about than that little troublemaker."

"He's a pain in the neck. I'll teach him a lesson when he gets back," the older man grumbled.

"Forget about it. Mako's waiting. Let's go inside."

"Fine, fine," the old man muttered, sounding like a kid who'd been told to eat his vegetables. He followed the other man into the power plant, the door creaking shut behind them.

Aya turned to Boubou, her eyes wide. "What do you think they're up to in there?"

Boubou shrugged, but his face was serious. "I don't know, but I have a feeling we're about to find out."

❖

As the men disappeared into the power plant, Djily shook his head. "Man, that old guy's got some serious anger issues."

Aya nodded, her face scrunched up in thought. "You got that right. Something's fishy about those two. They're about as trustworthy as a fox guarding a chicken coop."

Adama chimed in, his eyes still on the spot where the boy had vanished. "The kid seems okay, though. But man, those guys are treating him like yesterday's garbage."

Bouma's forehead wrinkled as he remembered something. "Didn't Toure say there were three guys running this joint?"

Boubou snapped his fingers, the pieces clicking into place. "They mentioned someone named Mako, remember? Bet you a week's allowance he's the third musketeer, hanging out inside the plant."

Aya's eyes lit up with that look that usually meant trouble (or adventure, depending on who you asked). "Let's go talk to the kid.

Maybe he can tell us what's really going on here. If these guys are inventors, I'm a monkey's uncle."

"Good idea," Boubou agreed, already starting to creep out from their hiding spot. "But let's be careful. We don't want to end up on the wrong side of that walking stick."

As they slowly made their way toward the back of the power plant, Djily whispered, "Is it just me, or does this whole thing feel like we're in some kind of weird mystery novel?"

Aya grinned, her eyes sparkling with excitement. "If we are, then I call dibs on being the brilliant detective who cracks the case!"

"As long as I'm not the first victim," Bouma muttered, making everyone stifle their laughter as they crept forward, ready to unravel the mystery of the not-so-inventive inventors and their cranky companion.

❖

The boy wandered along the old power plant's water channel, where the river rushed by, deep and fast. He shuffled on the worn wooden planks, hands stuffed in his pockets, looking like he had the weight of the world on his shoulders.

Djily watched him with a touch of sympathy. "Poor kid looks so lonely. They told him to go play, but it's like he doesn't even know how."

"We should talk to him," Boubou decided, already cooking up a plan. "If those grumpy guys come out and ask questions, we'll just pretend we're here on business, asking about battery prices or something."

Adama's eyes lit up. "That's perfect! My dad's a farmer, and he's always complaining about how much batteries cost. We've got flashlights all over the farm buildings that don't have power. It's a real pain. I can totally make up a believable story about that. It'll sound super legit!"

The siblings left their leafy hiding spot and crossed the overgrown area near the power plant's entrance. The boy by the water channel was lost in his own world and hadn't noticed them yet. He stood by the rushing water, occasionally glancing up at the constantly turning, water-splattered wheel.

Boubou voiced what he was thinking. "This whole patent battery thing is weird. There's been nothing about it on the news. Seems like only local farmers like Toure know about the old power plant's new business."

Djily offered his thoughts. "Maybe they're keeping it secret until everything's ready. Boubou, I bet you're already imagining some big mystery. But let's be real, we might just get told to scram."

Boubou shrugged, a casual smile on his face. "I'm not thinking it's some huge conspiracy or anything. Just curious about what's really going on here."

Bouma nodded in agreement. "Nothing wrong with that. If this long-lasting battery they're working on turns out to be a big deal, we'll be some of the first to know about it. How cool would that be?"

As they got closer to the wild power plant current, the boy finally looked up and saw them. He did look a bit like Aya Diouf, just as old Salimata Toure had said. But his face showed signs of a hard life; he looked thin and tired, with eyes that seemed way too sad for a kid his age.

"Looks like he hasn't had a good meal in forever," Aya said quietly, worry in her voice.

The boy, noticing them coming closer, started walking towards Boubou and Aya. But suddenly, everything went wrong. He stepped on a loose rock and lost his balance. The boy tried to steady himself, but it was no use. With a sharp yell, he fell backwards into the rushing water of the power plant channel.

"Help!" he screamed, his voice cutting through the air. "Help me!"

* * *

CHAPTER EIGHT

Waves Of Bravery

The river exploded into chaos so fast that Aya, Boubou, and their friends barely had time to blink. One second, everything was calm. The next? Total mayhem. It wasn't until they spotted a kid thrashing in the wild current that their brains caught up with their eyes.

Quick as lightning, Aya sprinted ahead, ditching her backpack mid-run. Beyond the old power plant, the river turned into a monster. Sharp rocks poked out everywhere, turning the water into a bubbling cauldron of doom. Anyone unlucky enough to get caught in there? Toast.

Her friends raced after her, worry etched on their faces. Weirdly, nobody at the power plant seemed to notice the drama unfolding. No alarms, no shouts, nada. It was like the river's roar had swallowed the kid's desperate cries whole.

"Help! Please!" The boy's voice was barely a squeak. He flailed wildly, each second dragging him closer to inevitable disaster.

"I can't swim!" he wailed, voice cracking like old paint.

Aya hit the riverbank at full speed. She took one look at the churning water and dove in like an Olympic champion. For a heart-stopping moment, she vanished under the froth. Then – pop! – she resurfaced just yards from the struggling kid.

The boy was in rough shape. He'd already gone under once, and his breathing sounded like a broken accordion. Just as he was about to sink again, Aya zoomed up like a torpedo and grabbed his collar.

The kid, panicking, tried to latch onto Aya like a terrified octopus. But she was ready for it. She knew how dangerous a drowning person's death grip could be. Skillfully, she kept just out of reach while maintaining her iron grip on his collar.

"Stay calm!" she yelled over the water's roar. "Just chill and hold on!"

Her words seemed to work magic. The boy stopped thrashing, making Aya's job a smidge easier. But they weren't out of the woods – or should we say, out of the rapids – yet.

The current was dragging them towards certain doom. Aya's eyes widened as she saw the Sharp Rock Obstacle Course of Death looming ahead. If they got sucked into that mess, game over.

With the boy in tow, Aya fought the current like it owed her money. She aimed for the shore, kicking and stroking with all her might. But it was like swimming through molasses. The current seemed to laugh at their efforts.

On the riverbank, her friends raced alongside, looking like they might throw up from worry.

"She's not gonna make it," Pierre muttered, his face as white as a ghost. "The current's way too strong."

Aya's face was a mask of pure determination as she battled the river's pull. The kid had started thrashing again, making her job even harder. Every second brought them closer to the Rapids of Doom, where the water turned into a whirlpool straight out of a nightmare.

Just ahead, a few rocks stuck out of the water like nature's lifelines. Beyond that? The river turned into a smooth, super-fast water slide, rushing towards a bend lined with droopy willows before dropping into a quarter-mile of rapids and waterfalls that would make even the bravest person wet their pants.

"I'm going in!" Boubou suddenly yelled, sounding like a superhero about to save the day.

He stopped at the edge, ready to dive. But Aya's hand found a rock just then, grabbing on for dear life. Adama, quick as a cat, grabbed Boubou's arm to stop him.

For a second, it looked like the current might rip Aya away from her rocky savior. But she held on like her life depended on it – because, well, it did. She hauled herself and the boy onto the rock with strength that would make a bodybuilder jealous.

The rock was wide and flat, barely underwater. Inch by inch, Aya dragged herself and the half-conscious kid onto this tiny island of hope. It wasn't much, but it was better than being fish food.

The boy was about as helpful as a sack of potatoes. He was barely awake, flopping around like a wet noodle. Aya almost had him on the rock when – oops! – her grip slipped. The current, sneaky as ever, yanked the kid sideways. His head went bonk against the rock, but Aya, moving faster than humanly possible, grabbed him before he could become a human boogie board.

Her fingers snagged his shirt just in time, pulling him back to their slippery sanctuary. The bonk had knocked the kid out cold. He lay there like a lump while Aya clung to him, both of them soaked to the bone.

"Get help!" she yelled to her friends, her voice raspier than sandpaper. "Find a rope!"

Boubou and Adama took off like rockets, sprinting towards the old power plant. Inside, it was business as usual – apparently, nobody had noticed the life-or-death drama happening right outside their windows.

They found the front of the power plant deserted.

"I'm going in," Boubou declared, sounding braver than he felt. "We need a rope, pronto, or they're both gonna end up downriver."

Time was ticking. Every second counted if they were going to save their friends from becoming the river's next victims.

❖

Boubou and Adama burst into the power plant like they were being chased by a pack of wild dogs. The inside was darker than a movie theater, totally different from the crazy scene outside. They'd barely taken two steps when – bam! – they crashed right into one of the workers they'd seen earlier. The guy looked like someone had just told him his hair was on fire.

"Whoa! What's the big idea?" he snapped, grabbing Boubou's shoulders like he was about to toss him out like yesterday's trash.

Just then, another worker came flying out of a nearby room, looking madder than a hornet with a stubbed toe.

"What in the world? Out! Now!" he barked, not even giving them a chance to explain.

Their yelling woke up a third guy who came stomping out of the shadows like an angry bear. He was built like a fire hydrant and was swinging a big stick around like he was trying to swat invisible flies. A dirty handkerchief around his neck made him look like a cranky cowboy.

"What's all this noise? What do you kids want?" he bellowed, his voice echoing off the walls.

"We need a rope," Boubou squeaked, trying to sound brave even though his knees were shaking. "There's a kid drowning in the river by the power plant!"

You could've heard a pin drop. The men's faces went from angry to shocked faster than you can say "Uh-oh."

"Which kid?"

"Where is he?"

"Why do you need a rope?"

The questions flew at Boubou like a flock of confused pigeons.

"He fell in, like, two minutes ago," Boubou explained, words shooting out of his mouth like a machine gun. "My sister just saved him, but they're stuck on a rock right by the rapids. If we don't hurry, they're gonna be goners. Please, we need a rope – now!"

"Mako, grab a rope! Move it!" the old guy with glasses yelled at the human fire hydrant.

Mako dropped his stick like it was on fire and zoomed back into the room he came from. He reappeared again in a flash, lugging a rope that looked strong enough to tie up an elephant.

"Alright, where are they?" the old man asked. "Show us, and step on it!"

❖

The power plant guys forgot all about being grumpy when they heard about the kid in trouble. Now, they were chasing after Adama and Boubou like they were in some crazy race. They all rushed to where the other boys were jumping up and down, yelling at Aya like cheerleaders gone wild.

Mako, the human fire hydrant, came huffing and puffing with the rope. The other boys stepped back, probably worried he might accidentally lasso one of them instead. He twirled the rope over his head like a cowboy, then flung it out towards Aya.

But... whoops! The rope fell short. Aya tried to grab it, but it was like trying to catch air. Mako's throw was about as accurate as a blindfolded archer.

"Move over, let me show you how it's done," the oldest guy grumbled, shoving Mako aside like he was rearranging furniture. He snatched up the rope, yanked it back from the river, and gave it another whirl.

The rope zoomed through the air like a snake with rocket boosters. It missed Aya's hand by a whisker and splashed into the water. But the old guy wasn't giving up. He reeled it back in, spun it around his head again, and sent it flying.

This time – bullseye! The rope landed right on Aya's shoulders. She grabbed it instantly, somehow managing to wrap it around herself while still holding onto the knocked-out kid. It was like watching a one-armed juggler, but she pulled it off with impressive skill.

The old guy watched, his face a mix of worry and excitement. He noticed the boy was as still as a statue, and Aya had to hold onto him like a slippery bar of soap.

"Kirabo!" he yelled, sounding like a worried grandpa. "Kirabo, can you hear me?"

"He bonked his head on a rock," Pierre chimed in, trying to sound cool and collected (and failing miserably). "Lights out. But I think he'll be okay."

❖

Suddenly, Aya looked up and waved, giving the "Let's do this!" signal. She hugged the boy tighter than a bear, then slid off the rock into the water like it was a weird waterpark ride.

The old guy, Boubou, and Mako grabbed the rope like they were playing tug-of-war with a giant. As Aya let go of her rocky lifesaver, they started pulling. When he saw how old and ratty the rope looked, Boubou's eyes got big as dinner plates. 'Oh man, I hope this thing holds,' he thought, his stomach doing backflips.

In the water, Aya and the out-cold kid bounced around like rubber ducks in a washing machine. Sometimes, they'd vanish completely under the waves, making everyone's hearts skip a beat. Inch by inch, they got closer to dry land.

But then - SNAP! The rope couldn't take it anymore. It broke apart like wet toilet paper, just yards away from safety.

The guys on the bank stumbled backward, looking as shocked as if they'd seen a ghost. The broken rope end whipped through the air like an angry snake.

In a moment that made time stand still, Aya and Kirabo were swept away by the river's angry current!

* * *

CHAPTER NINE

A Leap Of Faith

Boubou Diouf's quick-thinking brain had already cooked up a backup plan. He could tell the rope was about to snap any second. Just around the river bend, where the stream got skinny, and willow trees hung over the bank like long, green curtains, some nasty rapids were waiting. Boubou was ready to spring into action.

The instant the rope gave up, Boubou took off like a rocket. He zoomed along the riverbank towards the willows, his eyes glued to Aya. She was wrestling with the river like it was a cranky crocodile, and Boubou knew the clock was ticking. If the current swept them past the willows, it'd be game over. The rapids beyond were meaner than a handful of angry hornets.

Racing against Mother Nature herself, Boubou's mind was doing cartwheels. Could he reach the trees in time? Would the river play nice and bring Aya and Kirabo close enough to grab? Could he hold onto them without his arms turning into noodles? His brain was like a hamster on a high-speed wheel.

Suddenly, the riverbank decided to do a nosedive. Boubou sped down the grassy slope towards the willows, his heart doing the cha-cha in his chest. He was a smidge ahead of the two human rafts in the water, clinging to a teeny-tiny piece of hope that he could save his sister and the mystery boy.

Finally, he reached the willows. They were stretching over the river like they were trying to touch their toes in the water. Boubou grabbed hold of a tree and leaned out over the stream, feeling like a tightrope walker without a net.

Lady Luck must've been on lunch break, but she came back just in time – Aya was still a few yards upstream. But she was too far out, just beyond Boubou's reach as the river played keep-away.

Aya, the smart cookie she was, figured out Boubou's plan in a flash. She did her best to swim towards the shore, even though Kirabo was about as helpful as a sack of potatoes. Probably feeling a little guilty, the river decided to lend a hand. It curved near the bend, sending her right under the willow where Boubou was perched like a determined, human-shaped bird.

As Aya floated beneath him, Boubou stretched his arm so far he thought it might fall off. For a heart-stopping second, he was sure he'd missed. But then – bam! – their fingers connected like magnets. Boubou squeezed Aya's hand tighter than a jar of pickles.

The willow groaned like it was complaining about the extra weight, but Boubou held on like his life depended on it (which, you know, it kind of did). His arm muscles were screaming louder than a heavy metal band, and he knew he couldn't keep it up forever. But help was on the way, riding in like the cavalry.

Adama's voice cut through the chaos like a foghorn, "Hang on! We're coming!"

Boubou could hear him crashing through the bushes like a rhino in a china shop, with Pierre and the others hot on his heels.

With his friends' help, Boubou managed to haul Aya to safety, still holding onto Kirabo like he was an oversized, waterlogged teddy bear.

Soaked to the bone and looking like drowned rats, they all flopped onto the grass, panting like they'd just run a marathon.

They jumped into action, making sure Kirabo was okay. Lucky for him, aside from drinking half the river and getting his bell rung, he wasn't too worse for wear. After a bit, he started to come around, his eyes fluttering open like sleepy butterflies. The old man's face lit up like a Christmas tree while the other two men watched with poker faces.

Once Kirabo had enough juice to sit up, he wanted to know who his hero was. "Who saved me?" he asked, his voice as weak as a kitten's meow.

Boubou pointed at his sister with a grin. "Aya did," he said, puffing up like a proud peacock.

Wobbling to his feet, Kirabo gave Aya a bear hug that could've squeezed the water right out of her clothes. "I can't thank you enough," he said, his words dripping with gratitude. "I would've been fish food if not for you."

Aya, turning redder than a tomato with embarrassment, tried to dodge the spotlight. "Actually, it was him," she said, nodding at Boubou. "If he hadn't been there, we'd both be riding the rapids right now."

Kirabo then turned to Boubou, shaking his hand like he was trying to start a lawnmower. "Then I owe both of you a big thanks. You guys risked your necks for me."

The old man, who'd been watching everything go down, finally piped up. "It was mighty brave," he admitted, though he sounded about as excited as someone getting a root canal. "I'm grateful to you both for saving the boy. But listen up, Kirabo," he added, his voice sharp enough to cut glass, "stay away from that power plant race. I've told you a million times it's more dangerous than poking a sleeping lion. You might not get so lucky next time."

Kirabo, looking like a deflated balloon, mumbled, "I'm sorry, Uncle Dogo." His apology was heavier than an elephant on a seesaw.

❖

As the group trudged back to the power plant, Boubou and Aya couldn't help but notice the two men with Uncle Dogo looked about as welcoming as a pair of grumpy cats. It was crystal clear they wanted the kids to scram.

"Get the kid inside and dry him off," Mako grunted, jerking his head at Kirabo. "We've got work to do."

Aya, who was soaked to the bone herself, piped up hopefully, "Is there a fireplace inside?"

Uncle Dogo glanced at Mako, who shook his head like he was swatting a fly. "Nope," Uncle Dogo replied, short and not-so-sweet. "Kirabo can just hit the hay till his clothes dry out."

"I'm pretty soggy too," Aya pointed out, trying to get a little sympathy.

Mako ignored her like she was invisible and picked up the pace towards the power plant.

Boubou, feeling the tension thick as peanut butter, tried to change the subject. "So, when did you start running this joint?" he asked the old man.

"Couple weeks back," Uncle Dogo answered.

Adama, curious as a cat, said, "What's the scoop on your battery prices? My dad was just griping about how batteries cost an arm and a leg these days. He's always on the hunt for ones that don't die faster than a snowman in summer. He'd be here in a flash if he knew about this place. I bet he could really juice up your business."

Uncle Dogo looked as uncomfortable as a long-tailed cat in a room full of rocking chairs. He glanced at his buddy. "You should ask Keenan about that."

"Our prices are steep," Keenan said, flat as a pancake. "We're all about those fancy, long-lasting batteries."

"Don't you need customers for that?" Adama asked.

"We've got enough leads," Keenan brushed him off.

But Adama wasn't ready to throw in the towel. "So what exactly are these 'fancy, long-lasting battery' prices?"

After a pause longer than a commercial break, Keenan rattled off some prices that made the Zinguichor store look like a dollar shop.

"Whoa, that's way more than my dad would fork over," Adama said, deflating like a sad balloon.

Uncle Dogo just shrugged. "Take it or leave it. We're not begging for his business."

"At those prices, you definitely won't get it," Adama said.

It was clearer than a cloudless sky that Uncle Dogo and his pals weren't exactly rolling out the welcome mat for outsiders at their rusty old power plant. But Boubou figured they had every right to keep their operation under wraps, especially if they were cooking up some top-secret energy gadgets. Sensing they were treading on thin ice, he gave Adama a nudge that said, "Let's drop it."

❖

As they reached the crusty old power plant's entrance, Mako shooed Kirabo inside faster than a cat spotting a vacuum cleaner. Kirabo glanced back, his eyes screaming "thanks" one more time.

Keenan, eyeing the siblings like they were a puzzle he couldn't solve, asked, "Where are you kids from, anyway?"

"We live in Zinguichou," Boubou replied.

"That's a fair hike from here," Keenan said, his bushy eyebrows doing a little dance.

"Yeah, we're just out exploring," Boubou explained. "Thought we'd check out this neck of the woods."

"Better scoot if you don't want to miss dinner," Keenan hinted, about as subtle as a foghorn.

The siblings got the message loud and clear - these guys wanted them gone yesterday. Boubou, quick on the uptake, said, "Guess we'll hit the road then. We're gonna splash around in the river upstream. Aya can dry off her clothes there."

Suddenly remembering Aya's heroic rescue, Uncle Dogo dug into his pocket. "I'd like to give you something for saving Kirabo," he said, his gruff exterior cracking a bit.

Aya shook her head faster than a wet dog. As Uncle Dogo fished out two fifty-dollar bills, one for each sibling, Boubou and Aya waved them off, insisting they'd just done what any decent person would do.

But as Uncle Dogo held out the cash, Keenan let out a muffled yelp. Quick as a wink, he snatched the bills from Uncle Dogo and spun around. A heartbeat later, he turned back, offering the money again with a nervous chuckle.

"My bad," Keenan stammered, looking like he'd been caught with his hand in the cookie jar. "Thought he was only giving you ten bucks each. Fifty's right on the money. Go on, take it."

The siblings stood their ground despite Keenan pushing the cash like a used car salesman. Not wanting to make a bigger deal of it, Keenan pocketed the bills himself.

"Alright, if you won't take it, no use beating a dead horse," Keenan said, relief washing over him like a tidal wave. "But we really do appreciate what you did. Come on, Dogo, back to the grind," he added, changing gears faster than a race car driver.

Suddenly mute as a mime, Uncle Dogo turned and followed Keenan back into the spooky old power plant.

Watching them vanish, Aya whispered to Boubou, "Talk about giving us the bum's rush." She glanced at her soggy clothes with a sigh. "Let's head upriver. I can hang these duds out to dry. Better get that done before we trek back."

With that, the siblings set off, leaving the creepy power plant and its not-so-friendly residents in the dust, ready for whatever adventure the river had in store for them next.

✳ ✳ ✳

Mystery's Maiden Voyage

THE DAYS CRAWLED BY LIKE SLUGS ON A SIDEWALK. FOR A whole week, Boubou, Aya, and their friends had their noses buried in books, wrestling with stubborn historical dates and mind-bending geometry problems. Exams loomed over them like storm clouds, dark and menacing. Fun was a distant memory, even after school. They were all caught up in the familiar whirlwind of pre-exam panic, where everything they'd ever learned seemed to slip through their fingers like water. It felt like for every new fact they crammed into their brains, an old one got booted out.

Finally, the grueling week came to an end. On Saturday morning, Grandma Diouf peered over her book with a sly grin.

"So, what's the plan for today?" she asked, eyeing her grandkids.

Boubou slumped in his chair, his voice a mix of boredom and frustration. "Eh, nothing exciting. Might battle with geography for a bit, but honestly, I'm about ready to toss that book into outer space."

Stretching her arms dramatically, Aya said, "And I'm still stuck in algebra-land. But come on, it's such a perfect day outside. Plus, I've been glued to these books all week."

Their grandmother's eyes twinkled mischievously as she casually suggested, "How about a trip down to the harbor to shake things up?"

The siblings exchanged confused looks, then erupted into cheers that could wake the dead.

"The harbor? What for?" Boubou asked, puzzled but intrigued.

Little did they know, Grandma Diouf had cooked up a surprise that would knock their socks off. The kids had worked their tails off solving the Lighthouse diamond heist and putting a stop to those sneaky blood diamond smugglers. Their efforts hadn't just earned them a pat on the back – they'd scored a hefty reward, too. Being the sweethearts they were, they'd used the money to replace Pierre's dad's boat, never thinking to treat themselves.

Grandma Diouf remembered how their late father had always dreamed of buying a motorboat for the family. She decided it was high time these selfless kiddos got a reward of their own.

With a mischievous glint in her eye, Grandma Diouf turned back to her book, fighting to keep a straight face. "Why don't you two scoot down to the harbor? It's a perfect day for it," she said, cool as a cucumber.

The idea lit a fire under the siblings. In a whirlwind of flying shoes and slamming doors, they were out of the house, pedaling their bikes like they were in the Tour de France, and headed straight for Zinguichou. They had no clue that a jaw-dropping surprise awaited them at the harbor.

Behind the scenes, Grandma Diouf had been plotting like a master spy. She'd snagged a dock slip at the harbor, just a hop and a skip from their street. Her recent "administrative" trip to Zakar? All part of her grand master plan. As Boubou and Aya zoomed toward the harbor, they were blissfully unaware of the amazing revelation about to unfold before their eyes.

❖

As Boubou and Aya pedaled towards the harbor, everything suddenly clicked. "I bet Grandma's trip to Zakar wasn't just boring family stuff," Boubou said, his voice full of suspicion.

Aya grinned mischievously. "She was probably keeping us focused on studying. If we knew something big was coming, we'd have ditched those books in a heartbeat."

Boubou laughed. "Yeah, no kidding!"

The harbor was buzzing with activity when they reached the harbor, but they were laser-focused on their mission. As they raced to the end of the pier, their jaws nearly hit the ground.

The most fantastic motorboat they'd ever seen was there, bobbing in the water like a dream come true. It was sleek and white, with shiny gold details that sparkled in the sun. The boat looked built for speed and adventure. Flags fluttered proudly at both ends, and the leather seats looked incredibly comfortable. But the real kicker? The name on the side is in big, fancy letters: "MYSTERY." It was perfect – a name that matched their wildest dreams.

Boubou's eyes were wide with wonder. "Whoa! She's a beauty!"

"You can say that again!" Aya squealed. "It's the coolest boat in the whole bay!"

"And probably the fastest, too," Boubou said, practically bouncing excitedly.

As Boubou and Aya stood admiring the Mystery, an old fisherman with a weathered face and kind eyes approached them. His salt-and-pepper beard and well-worn cap spoke of years spent on the water.

"Ahoy there, young'uns," he said with a friendly wave. "You must be the Diouf kids."

Boubou and Aya exchanged puzzled glances before Aya replied, "Yes, we are. How did you know?"

The old fisherman's eyes twinkled. "Your grandmother asked me to keep an eye out for you. Said you'd be along this morning." He reached into his pocket and pulled out a sealed envelope. "She asked me to give you this when you arrived."

With trembling hands, Boubou took the envelope and carefully opened it. Inside was a letter written in their grandmother's elegant handwriting. As they read it together, their eyes widened in amazement:

"Dear Boubou and Aya,

This boat, the Mystery, is yours. It's a reward for your bravery and selflessness. You've shown courage beyond your years and kindness that warms my heart. May this vessel carry you to grand adventures and new discoveries.

Remember, true wealth lies not in possessions but in the love we share and the good we do for others. You've made me prouder than I can say.

All my love, Grandma."

Aya's eyes filled with tears of joy while Boubou swallowed hard, trying to contain his emotion. They looked at each other, then at the boat, then back at the letter.

"It's really ours," Aya whispered, her voice filled with awe and gratitude.

Boubou nodded, too overwhelmed to speak. This wasn't just any boat – it was a gift from their grandmother, a reward for their courage and kindness. The realization made the Mystery even more special, a symbol of their family's love and their own heroic deeds.

The old fisherman smiled warmly. "She's a beauty, that Mystery. Treat her well, and she'll take good care of you out there on the water."

With that, he tipped his cap and ambled away, leaving Boubou and Aya to marvel at their incredible gift and the adventures that it promised.

"Man, if we'd known about this all week, we wouldn't have learned a single thing at school!" Aya laughed.

They scrambled aboard the Mystery to check it out without wasting a second. It was even more awesome up close – the neatest, most compact, and beautiful motorboat they'd ever seen. Everything shone like it was brand new, and the wheel moved smoothly.

Boubou plopped into the driver's seat and asked, "How's the gas and oil situation?"

"All topped up," Aya replied, scanning the controls like a pro. "And look, Boubou, the license is already here!"

"Alright, let's go!"

Aya quickly untied the ropes and leaped aboard as Boubou fired up the engine. It coughed to life and purred as Boubou smoothly steered them out into the bay.

"This engine runs so smooth!" Boubou whooped. The siblings shared a look of pure joy as the Mystery glided over the water effortlessly.

Boubou's confidence at the helm of the Mystery wasn't just beginner's luck. Over the past few months, he had spent countless hours with Pierre and Mr. Leroy, soaking up their knowledge like a sponge. Mr. Leroy, a seasoned sailor, had taken Boubou under his wing, teaching him the ins and outs of boat handling. From mastering the throttle to navigating choppy waters, Boubou had learned it all.

Pierre, too, had shared his tricks for coaxing extra speed out of an engine. Those lessons had paid off, turning Boubou into a skilled young captain, ready to guide the Mystery through whatever adventures lay ahead.

As they looped back towards shore, the morning sun lit up the harbor, making several fancy motorboats gleam. A few of them were making a racket, sputtering and backfiring near the shore. Among these, they spotted a particularly cool new boat that caught their eye. They recognized it instantly as the replacement boat they'd generously bought for Pierre Leroy's dad.

"Hey, there's Pierre!" Boubou shouted, pointing at a familiar figure on the water. "He's always out here on Saturday mornings. Let's challenge him to a race!"

"I heard his is the fastest boat in the bay," Aya said, a competitive glint in her eye.

"I don't care if it is," Boubou declared boldly. "He'll have to really push it to beat the Mystery. Let's see what this baby can do!"

Pierre, busy fiddling with his boat, hadn't noticed who was cruising up in the new motorboat. As the Mystery pulled up beside him, he looked up in surprise.

"Holy moly!" he exclaimed, his face lighting up. "Look who it is! I was wondering who had the fancy new ride. Is this yours?"

"You bet it is," Aya replied with a proud grin. "And she's not just fast, she's lightning quick. Wanna race?"

Pierre's eyes sparkled at the challenge, and he laughed. "I'd hate to make you guys feel bad about your new toy by leaving you in my wake," he teased.

"You won't beat us," Boubou said with a confident smirk. "Your boat's quick, sure, but you've just met your match."

Pierre raised an eyebrow. "You think you can take me? This isn't just any boat—it's a real speed demon."

Boubou pointed towards a buoy bobbing in the distance. "Let's find out. We'll start from that buoy over there."

Both boats revved their engines, slicing through the water towards the buoy, neck and neck. As they reached it, Pierre yelled, "Go!"

In a flash, both boats shot forward. Pierre's boat roared, while the Mystery went from a gentle purr to a determined growl, cutting through the water with impressive speed.

Pierre, who knew every trick his boat could do, pushed it to the max, quickly pulling ahead. The Mystery trailed, but only for a moment. Boubou knew there was more power under the hood than it was letting on.

Slowly but surely, he coaxed more speed out of the Mystery, feeling the boat respond eagerly. They began to close the gap on Pierre's boat. Meanwhile, Pierre was going full throttle, his boat bouncing on the water's surface.

The race was on, and the two boats were tearing through the bay in a thrilling display of speed and skill. With Boubou at the helm, the Mystery proved to be more than a match for Pierre's celebrated speedster.

As the Mystery surged through the water, it quickly caught up with Pierre's zooming boat. In a smooth, fluid motion, it drew level with him. For a split second, the siblings caught sight of Pierre's face – a hilarious mix of shock and awe – as he glanced over at them in disbelief.

The Mystery kept charging ahead, slicing through the waves powerfully. Spray flew over its front as it rocked and swayed, showing off its speed and power. It was now crystal clear which boat was the champ; Pierre's craft was being left behind.

Once they were a good distance ahead – about three or four football fields – and it was obvious that Pierre had no chance of catching up, he slowed down his boat, admitting defeat. Boubou eased off the gas and smoothly turned the Mystery in a wide, graceful circle, cruising back to join Pierre at a more relaxed pace.

Pierre, still in shock from the unexpected turn of events, greeted them with a mix of amazement and respect. "I thought you were just kidding about racing me," he said as they got close.

Boubou grinned. "No joke about that race, huh?"

"You can say that again!" Pierre exclaimed, his voice carrying over the water. "I pushed my boat so hard I thought the engine might give out! Never dreamed there was a boat in the bay that could beat mine. But I guess your Mystery here is the new speed king. When did you guys get this beauty?"

"This is our first time out," Aya replied, her eyes shining with pride as she looked over the sleek lines of the Mystery.

Pierre looked on with a hint of envy. "Wish I could hang around for another round," he said, sounding bummed. "But I've got to head back. I promised my dad I'd help him at the office this morning."

"That's a bummer," Boubou sympathized. "Maybe we'll catch up later. But we're gonna take it easy on the engine for a bit. Pushing it that hard on its first run probably wasn't the smartest move."

Pierre nodded, curiosity piqued. "Where are you guys off to now?"

"Just cruising around," Boubou replied casually. "Thinking of heading up the Cazamoun River, maybe as far as Zabrousse and back."

"That's a decent trip," Pierre mused. "Should take you about half an hour if you keep it steady. Though with that speedster, you could probably make it much quicker!"

Aya chuckled, "We'll stick to a slower pace. Don't want to overdo it on our first day out."

Pierre gave a nod of approval. "Seems like she runs great. But yeah, better not push your luck. I gotta head off now. Catch you later!"

With a final wave, Pierre steered his boat back towards the harbor, the engine humming as he sped away. The Diouf siblings, meanwhile, set their course in the opposite direction, the Mystery's engine purring as they made their way toward the calm waters near Zabrousse.

CHAPTER ELEVEN

Journey Interrupted

Nestled along the sun-kissed shores of the same name, the quaint fishing village of Zabrousse sat just a few miles from the bustling town of Zinguichou. For most folks, Zabrousse was just another dot on the map, but for Boubou and Aya, it was the gateway to their own slice of paradise – a secret beach where their imaginations could run wild.

That morning, as they set sail for Zabrousse, the sky was a perfect canvas of blue. But Boubou, ever the watchful captain, noticed dark clouds sneaking in from the horizon. The wind picked up, whistling a warning tune. Coastal storms had a habit of popping up like uninvited guests, but Boubou wasn't worried. He knew they'd have the wind at their backs for the return trip – a comforting thought as the storm brewed its mischief.

Their trusty boat, the Mystery, cut through the waves like a hot knife through butter. Its engine purred contentedly, barely disturbing the water's surface. Boubou and Aya felt like they were gliding on glass, lost in their own world. In that moment, perched on their beloved vessel, they wouldn't have traded places with anyone – not even a king on his golden throne.

By the time they docked at Zabrousse, the sky had transformed into a moody grey blanket. Without a word, the siblings agreed this would be a quick pit stop. The village hummed with its usual morning bustle as they stretched their sea legs on the wharf. They couldn't help but notice the approving looks thrown at the Mystery.

Two weathered fishermen, their skin as wrinkled as old maps, lounged on the wharf, their feet dangling above the lapping waves. They eyeballed the Mystery from bow to stern, nodding appreciatively.

"Well, slap me with a jellyfish!" exclaimed the first fisherman, his voice as gravelly as the beach. "That's one fine boat, eh, Omar?"

His companion, Omar, squinted at the Mystery. "You're not wrong, Demba. Sleek as a dolphin and probably twice as smart. Unlike some captains I know," he added with a sly grin.

Demba clutched his chest in mock offense. "Are you calling me a flounder-brain again?"

"If the fin fits," Omar chuckled, ducking to avoid a playful swat from his friend.

With the Mystery given their seal of approval (no small feat in these parts), the old-timers reloaded their pipes. Boubou and Aya listened in, captivated by these walking encyclopedias of nautical lore and their colorful banter.

Boubou's eyes drifted to the darkening sky. "Looks like we're in for some weather," he murmured, nudging Aya. His words snapped her out of her story-induced trance. She loved these colorful yarns, each one wilder than the last. But one look at the brooding horizon told her Boubou was right. Time to head back to Zinguichou, and fast.

As they prepared to leave, Demba said, "You kids be careful out there. The sea's got more mood swings than my wife during mango season!"

"Demba!" Omar elbowed his friend but couldn't hide his own grin. "Don't mind him. Just remember, if the waves get too frisky, just wink at 'em. Works every time!"

Boubou and Aya laughed, waving goodbye to the jovial pair as they cast off, the fishermen's hearty chuckles fading behind them. The siblings settled into their familiar routine, preparing for what they thought would be an uneventful trip.

❖

As Boubou reached for the rope to secure their belongings, an unexpected commotion erupted on the shore. A man, seemingly in a great hurry, came sprinting down the road toward the dock. He was a flurry of motion, arms waving, voice loud and urgent.

"Hey! Wait!" he shouted, his voice cutting through the quiet of the wharf.

Boubou and Aya paused, exchanging curious glances before turning toward the newcomer. This wasn't part of their plan, but something about the man's desperation caught their attention.

"What's going on?" Aya whispered to her brother as they watched the stranger approach.

Boubou shrugged, his hand still on the rope. "No idea, but it looks like our quiet day just got a lot more interesting."

The man skidded to a stop at the edge of the dock, panting heavily. He was a sight to behold - stout and thick-set, with uniquely braided hair that made him stand out in their familiar surroundings. He looked like he'd run a marathon, gasping for breath as he reached them.

"Whew!" he huffed, dabbing his forehead with a brightly colored silk handkerchief. "Thought I'd miss you."

Boubou, always the more direct of the two, got straight to the point. "What's up? What do you need?"

The man's request was straightforward, albeit a bit odd. "Need a lift to Zinguichou, and fast. There's a train I can't miss. Get me there in twenty minutes, and I'll make it worth your while - how does fifty bucks sound?"

Boubou and Aya shared a doubtful look. They knew the train schedules like the back of their hands, and nothing matched his urgency. But the man was earnest, almost desperate, waving the money as if it was a white flag.

"Come on, what do you say?" he pressed, a hint of impatience creeping into his voice. "Twenty minutes to Zinguichou. There's easy money in it for you."

"Fifty bucks, huh?" Boubou mused later, a hint of amazement in his tone. "That's not something you come across every day." Their grandmother, ever the practical one, had given them the Mystery with one clear rule: no dipping into their savings for fuel. So, every dollar for their boating adventures was hard-earned and carefully spent.

"Alright, hop in," Boubou said with a decisive nod. "Twenty minutes to Zinguichou? We've got this."

"Thank you," the man replied, relief washing over his face as he climbed aboard. "Please, as fast as you can."

Boubou slid into the driver's seat, and the Mystery's engine soon roared to life. They pulled away from the wharf, the boat swiftly cutting a path through the bay. The Mystery seemed to sense the urgency, her speed steadily increasing until the salty spray danced around them, a testament to their swift journey toward Zinguichou.

Their mysterious passenger leaned back, looking grateful and relieved.

"You don't know how lucky I feel finding you guys," he shared. "I was almost convinced I'd be stuck there. The only ride in town was this old clunker that looked like it would fall apart if you sneezed at it. Seeing your boat was like spotting a lifesaver."

They kept close to the shoreline as they zipped across the water, the Mystery slicing through the waves under the increasingly overcast sky. This route was strategic—it shaved off precious minutes on their way to Zinguichou and offered a clear view of the coastal road just above the beach.

Aya, ever observant, noticed the man's attention was frequently drawn to the shore. His glances were more than just casual; they were filled with anxiety. Then, his face suddenly tightened with alarm. Following his gaze, Aya spotted two figures on the road. They were running, arms flailing in the air, clearly desperate to catch someone's attention.

"Looks like someone's trying to flag us down," she remarked to Boubou, tension in her voice.

"Those guys friends of yours?" Boubou said casually, turning back to their passenger.

The man's response came with a laugh, an attempt to sound nonchalant, but it didn't quite mask his underlying nervousness. "Yeah, they're buddies of mine," he confessed, trying to maintain a light tone. "Pulled a fast one on them, it seems." His chuckle sounded more forced than amused. "They've just figured out I've dodged them."

Boubou, sensing there was more to the story, pressed further. "So, what's going on? Why the great escape?"

"That was quite the trick I pulled," the stranger said, his laughter echoing a bit too heartily over the sound of the boat's engine. "Here's the deal – I'm getting married. That's why this train is a must for me. I kept it a secret until today, but somehow, my pals caught on. They decided to pull a prank on me. I left early, but they messed with my car's engine. It died on me, and I had to run back to town. They thought they had me cornered, but I showed them. I outsmarted them alright."

He laughed again, a bit too forcefully. The siblings exchanged a look; something about his laugh, a bit too strained, too eager, didn't sit right with them.

Boubou's eyes drifted back to the two men on the road. Their frantic gestures seemed excessive for just a prank. They were still desperately waving, signaling for the boat to return. Something didn't add up.

Boubou leaned closer to Aya, his voice low. "This doesn't make sense. I can't think of any train leaving Zinguichou around now. Something's off here."

"Yeah," Aya whispered back, her eyes narrowing in thought. "If this was just a joke, they'd have given up by now, not running around like the world's ending."

Boubou nodded, his mind racing. "The whole thing's off. He was too desperate to leave town and fast."

"I'm thinking we should head back. This could drag us into something we don't want," Aya suggested, concern in her voice.

"And if we do, he's going to flip," Boubou added. "We can just tell him we don't want his cash and drop him off where we found him."

Boubou turned to their passenger, his tone casual yet probing. "So, what time's this train of yours supposed to leave?"

The man's response came quickly, a bit too quickly. "About ten-thirty."

Boubou shook his head, his voice firm. "No train from Zinguichou leaves at that time."

The man seemed rattled now, his composure slipping. "But that's when my train's scheduled!"

Aya chimed in, reinforcing her brother's point. "The first train's not until noon."

The stranger was insistent, almost frantic. "I'm telling you, my train's at ten-thirty. I have to make it."

Boubou's decision was clear, his tone resolute. "Sorry, but it looks like you'll miss it. We're heading back to town."

The man's reaction was immediate, a mix of surprise and panic. "Turn back? Why on earth would you do that?"

Boubou's response was calm yet unyielding. "Something about this doesn't sit right with us. Those guys on the shore are way too worked up for this to be just a prank."

"They're just trying to reel us back in so they can have their laugh," the man argued, his voice laced with desperation.

Boubou was resolute. "Looks like they'll have their moment either way. We've decided not to go to Zinguichou. And about your offer of fifty bucks? We're not interested."

The man's agitation spiked. "You have to take me! I need to be on that train."

Boubou's patience was wearing thin. "Listen, this is our boat. We call the shots. We didn't have to agree to take you in the first place."

The stranger was becoming increasingly frantic. "But you said you'd take me! I need to make that train!"

Boubou stood firm, his voice calm but firm. "There's no train leaving at ten-thirty. We're heading back to town. You'll still have time to catch the noon train."

The stranger's frustration was palpable, his teeth clenched in annoyance. He started to rise, a move born of anger, before sinking back into his seat, seemingly aware he was overstepping his bounds.

"What a joke," he snarled bitterly. "You drag me out here, then decide to turn back."

Boubou glanced at him, then back at the shore. "Seems like your pals are pretty eager to catch up with you for some reason."

With a firm grip on the wheel, Boubou started maneuvering the Mystery, preparing to change course back to town. That's when they heard the stranger's harsh, demanding voice right behind them.

"Don't you dare turn this boat around! Keep going to Zinguichou!"

Boubou and Aya whirled around, shock etched on their faces. The man had risen to his feet, looming over them, a gun in his hand pointed directly at the siblings. The friendly façade was gone, replaced by a look of desperation and danger.

CHAPTER TWELVE

Lost In The Fog

BOUBOU AND AYA DIOUF'S PEACEFUL BOAT TRIP TOOK A sudden, heart-pounding turn. Their jaws dropped as they stared at the shiny revolver pointed their way. The stranger's face was as hard as stone, making it clear he wasn't joking around.

"Turn this boat to Zinguichou," he ordered, his voice as cold as the metal in his hand. "And don't try anything silly, got it?"

Boubou, trying to sound brave despite his racing heart, sputtered, "What's going on? Why Zinguichou?"

"I need to get there, and you two are my ticket," the stranger growled. He tapped the gun, making the siblings flinch. "This persuader here is loaded. Don't play hero, kids."

Boubou and Aya shared a worried glance, having a silent conversation with their eyes. The stranger let out a chuckle that sent shivers down their spines.

"Let's keep this simple," he continued. "I've got a train to catch and a wedding to attend. Can't be late, you see. Turning this boat around would be a big mistake. I don't usually carry this thing, but today's my lucky day. Don't push me."

His attempt to lighten the mood fell flat, and his steely gaze made his threat crystal clear. Boubou looked at Aya, hoping she had a brilliant idea hidden up her sleeve.

"Guess we don't have much choice," Boubou grumbled, shoulders slumping. "I'm not in the mood for bullet holes today."

"Yeah, that gun's not leaving much room for witty comebacks," Aya agreed, her usual spark dimmed by worry. "Let's just get Mr. Trigger-happy to Zinguichou and call it a day."

With a heavy sigh, Boubou spun the wheel. The boat cut through the waves, now heading straight for Zinguichou.

"We're taking you to the city," Boubou told the stranger, trying to sound tough. "But just so you know, if we see even a tiny chance, we're turning you in to the police. This whole gun-waving business? It's not cool. It's basically robbery."

"You might change your tune once we reach Zinguichou," the man said with a smirk. "After the wedding, I'll have my new wife send you a thank-you card. Trust me, I'm not a fan of using this gun, but missing that train? Not an option."

Boubou and Aya weren't buying the stranger's story about catching a train. Now that he'd forced them to take him to Zinguichou at gunpoint, they were even more suspicious.

"If only we could grab that gun somehow," Boubou whispered to Aya as he steered the boat.

Aya shook her head slightly. "Fat chance. His eyes are glued to us like we're the last slice of pizza."

"Plotting to snatch my gun, are we?" the stranger interrupted, his voice dripping with mock amusement. "Save your energy, kids. I'm running this show."

"We know that," Boubou snapped back, frustration evident in his voice. "But just wait till we get to Zinguichou. Things might not go the way you planned, Mr. Train Chaser."

❖

Dark storm clouds loomed over the bay as the Diouf siblings' boat, the Mystery, sliced through the choppy waters. The sky looked like it was throwing a temper tantrum, and the sea wasn't far behind. The water had turned a moody slate-gray, churning with white-capped waves that seemed determined to give them a wild ride.

"Looks like we're in for some serious weather," Boubou said, his voice barely louder than the waves. "Maybe it's a good thing we didn't turn back after all."

As if on cue, lightning crackled across the sky like a giant sparkler, followed by a rumble of thunder that sounded like the sky's stomach growling. The Mystery was holding up okay against the choppy waters, but it was starting to feel like they were on a water-based rollercoaster.

After a few minutes of this aquatic rodeo, Boubou snuck a peek over his shoulder. What he saw almost made him burst out laughing. Their gun-waving passenger, who'd been so tough and scary before, had turned into a green-faced mess. He was slumped against the cushions, still clutching the revolver but looking like he was about to lose his breakfast, lunch, and maybe even tomorrow's dinner.

It took Boubou a second to connect the dots. Then, as the boat took an especially wild dip, it hit him like a water balloon to the face. He gave Aya a nudge that was about as subtle as an elephant trying to tiptoe.

"He's getting seasick," Boubou whispered to Aya, trying his best not to grin like the Cheshire Cat.

Aya took a quick look and bit her lip to keep from giggling. The guy who'd been so menacing before now looked about as threatening as a wet noodle.

"Go faster, will you?" the stranger croaked, waving the gun with all the strength of a limp spaghetti strand.

Boubou, being the oh-so-helpful captain, cranked up the speed. The boat started bouncing even more, like a rubber duck in a washing machine.

"Yeah, that's... that's better," the man mumbled, not sounding convinced at all. In fact, he sounded like he was trying to convince his stomach to stay put.

"I've got an idea," Boubou whispered to Aya, his eyes twinkling with more mischief than a class clown on April Fool's Day. Suddenly, he yanked the wheel, turning the boat sideways to the waves.

"Hey—what gives?" the stranger yelped, his voice a mix of alarm and nausea. "Why are we changing direction?"

"Just adjusting our course," Boubou said, cool as a cucumber in a freezer. "Heading towards the shore a bit, away from the wind."

The stranger bought it hook, line, and sinker, but he was looking worse by the second. The Mystery was now taking on the waves like a champ, but the up-and-down motion was about as soothing as a pogo stick marathon for their queasy passenger.

"He's definitely losing it," Aya whispered, trying not to sound too amused at their captor's misery.

Boubou grinned at Aya like he'd just thought of the world's best prank. "Watch this," he said. He jerked the wheel again, making the boat cut across the waves at a sharp angle.

That did it. The stranger groaned louder than a zombie with a stubbed toe, slumping forward with his head in his hands.

Aya saw her chance and pounced like a cat on a mouse. Quick as lightning, she leaped up and knocked the gun out of the man's hand. It flew through the air in a graceful arc and plopped into the water with a satisfying splash.

But the stranger wasn't ready to wave the white flag just yet. He swung at Aya, catching her on the cheek with a blow that would've made a boxer proud. Aya stumbled but came right back at him like a rubber band. They wrestled around the boat, looking like a weird dance duo on the world's shakiest dance floor.

Boubou saw Aya was in trouble and jumped in to help faster than you can say "sibling rescue squad." He wrapped his arm around the stranger's neck, trying to pull him off his sister. The man fought back hard, landing a punch on Boubou's ribs that made him gasp like he'd just jumped into an ice-cold pool.

In the chaos, the stranger reached into his pocket and tossed something overboard. But Boubou didn't have time to play "guess what's in the water." He steadied himself on the rocking boat and, with timing that would've made a kung-fu master proud, landed a solid punch right on the guy's jaw.

The punch didn't knock him out, but it sent him stumbling like a newborn giraffe on roller skates. His head bonked against the side of the boat with a thud that sounded like a coconut hitting the ground, and down he went, out cold.

"Aya, tie him up," Boubou said, catching his breath. "Use that rope over there. I need to get us back on course before we end up in Timbuktu or something."

But as Boubou retook the wheel, he realized they had a problem bigger than a whale in a kiddie pool. A thick fog had rolled in, turning the world into a giant marshmallow. Zinguichou had vanished like it was playing the world's biggest game of hide-and-seek.

"Aya, you don't happen to have a compass hidden in your pocket, do you?" Boubou asked, hope in his voice.

Aya looked up from tying the stranger's ankles. "Nope, sorry. Fresh out of magical direction-finding devices. Isn't there one on the boat?"

Boubou sighed like he'd just been told homework was invented. "No, there isn't. And now we're lost in this fog soup. I'm not even sure if we're heading towards Zinguichou or sailing off to who-knows-where! We could end up discovering a new continent at this rate!"

∗ ∗ ∗

CHAPTER THIRTEEN

Toto Panko

Boubou eased off the throttle of the motorboat, his eyes straining to see through the thick fog that surrounded them. Danger lurked in the misty blanket - they could crash into another boat or smash against the sharp rocks along the shore at any moment.

The fog was like a giant cotton ball, making it impossible to see. Boubou tried to steer by feeling the direction of the waves, but it was tricky with the swirling currents and shifting wind.

The Mystery inched forward, gliding almost blindly through the hazy bay. Boubou squinted, hoping for any sign of land.

Meanwhile, Aya finished tying up the stranger, who was starting to wake up. His eyes fluttered open with a groan.

"Had enough excitement for one day?" Aya asked, her voice a mix of concern and sass.

"Who hit me?" the man mumbled, clearly confused.

"You hit yourself, genius. Smacked your head on the boat. Planning any more bright ideas?" she asked, eyeing him suspiciously.

The man groaned again and tried to sit up, only to realize he was tied up. He flopped back down with a dramatic sigh.

"He's not going anywhere now," Aya said, moving towards Boubou. The fight had clearly gone out of their unwanted passenger.

Boubou, still at the wheel, let out a frustrated huff. "I wish this fog would just disappear," he grumbled.

As if by magic, a sudden gust of wind blew through, lifting the foggy curtain for a split second. In that brief moment, Boubou caught a glimpse of Zinguichou straight ahead. He quickly spotted the lighthouse and adjusted their course.

The fog swallowed them up again, but Boubou felt more confident. "We're on the right track now," he announced, relief in his voice.

Aya peered into the mist. "Think we can find the pier? I can barely see my hand in front of my face."

Boubou nodded. "Good point. Let's aim for the big ferry dock instead. It's harder to miss."

Slowly, the Mystery crept through the fog, passing ghostly shapes of other boats near Zinguichou's wharf. The city loomed ahead like a spooky shadow.

Finally, they steered into one of the slips at the wharf. To their surprise, they could make out several figures hurrying along the dock, their shapes blurred by the mist.

"What boat is that?" a voice called out.

"It's the Mystery!" Boubou shouted back.

"Good! That's them. I thought they'd come here," the voice said, clearly relieved.

As the Mystery docked, Aya noticed the figures on the wharf. "Looks like we've got a welcome party," she remarked.

As one of the figures got closer, they realized it was someone they knew - it was their Grandmother!

"Grandma!" Aya called out, surprised and happy to see her.

Grandma Diouf got right to the point. "Do you have him with you?" she asked urgently.

"Who, Boubou?" Aya asked, confused.

"No, no. The man from Zabrousse village. I got a call about him."

"Yeah, he's here," Boubou chimed in. "He tried to use a gun on us, but we handled it."

"Good job," Grandma Diouf said proudly, peering into the boat at the messy-looking stranger trying to sit up.

"Alright, Chief!" she called out to Chief Gaye, the round Chief of Police of Zinguichou, who was huffing and puffing his way down the dock with Detective Diallo, his tall and skinny assistant.

"Got him, did you?" Chief Gaye wheezed.

"Yes, he's in the boat," Grandma confirmed.

"Great. Hand him over then," the Chief directed as he and Detective Diallo got ready to take the stranger.

As Boubou and Aya untied the ropes around the stranger's ankles, they wondered how their Grandmother knew about their unexpected passenger and why the police were already there. They helped the man over the side of the boat and watched as the officers quickly grabbed him and started searching him.

"Hey, what's the big idea?" the man protested, looking confused.

Chief Gaye puffed up importantly. "Thought you'd given us the slip, eh, Toto Panko?"

"You've got the wrong guy," the man mumbled.

"No mistake here," Chief Gaye said confidently. "Word is you were busy 'pushing paper' in Zabrousse village this morning."

Boubou and Aya exchanged glances, remembering their dad explaining that 'pushing paper' was slang for using fake money.

"The Secret Service almost caught you. Lucky for you, these kids' boat was there," Chief Gaye continued. He then turned to Boubou and Aya, trying to look important. "So, what story did this character spin for you two?"

Boubou answered, "He said he had to catch a train for his wedding. Claimed his friends were trying to stop him as a joke."

"We didn't really buy it, and we were about to turn back when he pulled a gun on us," Aya added dramatically.

"And how on earth did you two manage to overpower him?" Chief Gaye asked, eyebrows raised.

"Well, the guy got super seasick, and Aya here was quick enough to knock the gun out of his hand. That's when we jumped him," Boubou explained with a little smirk.

"Well done," Grandma Diouf said, sounding proud and relieved. "This morning, I got a call from some Secret Service agents. They've been chasing Toto Panko for a while. They almost caught him when he suddenly ran off. They chased him down the street, but he vanished into thin air. Next thing they knew, he was on your boat, heading for Zinguichou. They tried to get your attention from the beach—"

"That explains those two guys we saw running along the shore!" Aya interrupted, putting the pieces together.

"But since you didn't turn back, they figured out whose boat 'The Mystery' was. Luckily, the local fishermen in Zabrousse knew you two and told the agents. So, they called me to stop your boat and catch him. I was just about to call the police when—" Grandma Diouf was cut off by Chief Gaye.

"I'll take it from here, Mrs. Diouf," Chief Gaye butted in impatiently. He then turned to Diallo, who was patting down Panko. "Find anything on him?" he asked.

Detective Diallo stood up, scratching his head. "Nothing much. Just a hundred-dollar bill and some regular matches."

"No fake money?" Chief Gaye asked, sounding surprised.

"Not a single bill."

"That's weird. The Secret Service guys said he had a bunch of counterfeit cash on him."

"That explains it!" Boubou exclaimed, his eyes lighting up. "While we were wrestling with him on the boat, he pulled something out of his pocket and threw it overboard. I was too busy to think about what it might be."

"Looks like he got rid of the evidence," Chief Gaye mused, looking at Toto Panko, who stood there glumly with his pockets turned out. "What's your story, Panko?"

"I've got nothing to say. You can't prove anything."

"Maybe not right now," Chief Gaye shot back. "But just wait until those Secret Service agents get here from Zabrousse. We hear you've been passing fake money around the village."

Panko, the prisoner, quickly said, "Any fake money I might've used, I got from someone else. I'm not part of that gang."

Grandma Diouf turned to Boubou and Aya and said, "He's not the same guy who tricked you with that fake fifty-dollar bill at the train station, is he?"

Both grandchildren nodded and said, "No, Grandma, it's not him."

Chief Gaye, eager to show he was in charge, quickly added, "Either way, I bet this guy's mixed up with that criminal gang somehow."

Panko stubbornly insisted, "You can't prove anything. Sure, I might have accidentally used some fake bills in the village. But if I did, it wasn't my fault. Someone else gave me that money."

Chief Gaye, not buying it, pressed further, "If you're so innocent, why did you run when the detectives showed up?"

"I had a train to catch," Panko said weakly.

Detective Diallo scoffed, "Save it for the judge. I think it's time for you to cool off in a cell for a while, think about what you've done."

"Yeah, let him chill out behind bars," Chief Gaye added with a smug grin.

✳ ✳ ✳

CHAPTER FOURTEEN

The Bell That Rang Chaos

Detective Diallo felt like he was on top of the world. His heart was bubbling with happiness, and his stomach was comfortably full. The sun painted everything with a warm glow, and to make things even better, one of the local officials had just given him a pretty nice cigar. For a whole week, his usual routine had been blissfully quiet, free from any criminal shenanigans. Adding to his good mood, his wife was away visiting her sister in the countryside. This left Detective Diallo enjoying a rare moment of peaceful solitude as he strolled along on his patrol.

Even those pesky siblings, who usually drove him crazy, hadn't bothered him in days. He wondered if they might be buried under a mountain of textbooks, cramming for exams. "If that's what's keeping them out of my hair, then exams are the best thing ever," Diallo thought with a chuckle. He wished they happened more often if it meant some peace and quiet for him.

As he walked down Main Street, Diallo was the picture of relaxation. He lazily swung his baton while sticking to the cooler, shaded side of the street. Every so often, he'd tip his hat and reply with a solemn "Good afternoon" to the friendly nods and greetings from people passing by. These moments made him think there weren't many jobs better than being Deputy of the Zinguichou police force. He felt pretty good about where he was in life.

He exchanged a quick nod and hello with Officer Boubacar Sarr, who was stuck directing traffic at the not-so-busy main intersection. Diallo couldn't help but feel a bit smug that he wasn't stuck with that job. Traffic duty meant dealing with all kinds of nasty weather, from freezing, soaking rains to the kind of heat that made the pavement sizzle. Nope, he thought with a smile, patrolling the beat was definitely the way to go.

As Detective Diallo continued his walk, he spotted a group of boys from Zinguichou High School heading his way. He tensed up automatically; those Diouf siblings were always causing him headaches with their clever schemes.

He noticed the siblings among their friends and frowned. The Dioufs were too smart for their own good. He grudgingly admitted they weren't exactly troublemakers, but they had a knack for sticking their noses into police business. Twice now, they'd managed to solve mysteries that Detective Diallo was sure he could have cracked himself if he'd had a little more time.

Then, there was Amath, the prank ringleader, a boy who seemed destined for mischief. Detective Diallo couldn't shake the feeling that Amath and his crew – Adama, Pierre, Bacary, Djily, and Bouma – were all heading for trouble.

Despite this, Detective Diallo was in such a good mood that afternoon that he decided to nod at the group as he passed. To his surprise, the siblings and their friends actually gathered around him.

"What's the deal with Toto Panko?" Boubou asked, his eyes sparkling with curiosity.

Detective Diallo put on his most serious crime-fighting face and replied, "He's sitting in jail, and that's where he's going to stay for a while."

"Hasn't he gone to trial yet?" Boubou pressed.

The Detective shook his head. "Not yet. That troublemaker managed to get a lawyer, so they've pushed back the court date."

Amath, who was casually holding a package wrapped in brown paper, chimed in, "So, he's probably looking at some serious jail time, huh?"

"You bet," Detective Diallo confirmed with a nod.

Then, sounding casual, Amath turned to the Diouf siblings and asked, "Didn't you guys say once that Chief Diallo was the one who caught this counterfeiter?"

Detective Diallo couldn't help but puff up a bit when he heard Amath call him "Chief Diallo." The idea that these kids thought he played a big part in catching Panko was too good to ignore. Trying to act humble (which didn't come naturally to him), he waved off the compliment.

"I did my part," he admitted, trying to sound modest but not quite hiding the pride in his voice.

Aya, always quick to spice up a story, smoothly added, "Without Detective Diallo, Panko might have slipped right through our fingers. You should've seen it! He slapped those handcuffs on that crook so smoothly at the dock. It was like he was waiting there just for us."

Detective Diallo beamed at this, enjoying the slightly exaggerated praise. It made him rethink his opinion of these youngsters. Maybe they weren't just troublemakers after all, but bright, insightful kids who could spot real talent and even look up to him as a kind of father figure.

"That's right," he said, trying to sound serious, "I made sure Panko got behind bars, and trust me, he's not getting out anytime soon."

Detective Diallo said this as if he had single-handedly caught Panko and was personally keeping him locked up. It was a stretch, but he couldn't help enjoying the moment.

"No way Panko's getting past you, Chief Diallo," Amath said, his eyes twinkling.

Diallo felt a surge of respect for Amath, even if the boy had gotten his rank wrong. "Well, actually, I'm a Detective," he corrected, sounding a bit sad. "Not the Chief—just the Deputy Detective."

Amath pretended to be shocked. "What? You're not the Chief?"

"Not yet," Diallo replied, hinting that his promotion to Chief was just a matter of time.

Amath turned to his friends, looking like he couldn't believe it. "Can you believe this?" he exclaimed. "Here's Detective Diallo, a real sharp mind, walking the beat while someone like Gaye gets to be Chief. It's just not fair. Not fair at all." The way Amath said 'Detective' Diallo and 'Chief' Gaye, it was clear he was playfully questioning why things were the way they were in the police force.

The Diouf siblings nodded solemnly, all agreeing that it wasn't right.

"A man's just got to be patient," Diallo said, trying to sound like someone who'd been through a lot of tough times.

"But there's only so much waiting a person can do!" Amath burst out. "They're not appreciating you, Mr. Diallo. If I were you, I'd stand up for what I deserve."

Diallo tried to sound mysterious as he replied, "Oh, I'll get my chance."

"You bet you will. And we're going to make it happen sooner rather than later. Let's spread the word, guys. We need to get people talking. If everyone starts saying Detective Diallo should be promoted, then it's bound to happen."

Diallo couldn't help but feel a bit proud of this. "Well, I must say, a little push in the right direction wouldn't hurt."

"Consider it done," Amath promised, nodding seriously. "You can count on us, Mr. Diallo. We'll make sure everyone knows how great you are at your job. You're the one to shake things up around here."

Detective Diallo, feeling a bit overwhelmed by all this praise but secretly agreeing with every word of it, beamed with pride and gratitude.

"I never knew you kids thought so highly of me," he said, looking genuinely surprised. "I always figured you had some kind of problem with me."

The siblings quickly assured him they felt no such thing.

"Maybe we've been a bit of a handful sometimes," admitted Amath, sounding a little sorry. "But that's only because we didn't really understand you. From now on, you can count on us, Mr. Diallo. Your time to shine is coming."

With a flourish, Amath brought out the package he'd been carrying. "Hey, Mr. Diallo, would you mind keeping an eye on this for me? You'll be around here for another ten minutes, right?"

Diallo looked a bit suspicious. "Why can't your friends hold onto it?"

"Well, we're all sticking together, and it's just a pain to carry around. If a guy named Moussa comes by asking for it, could you give it to him?"

Diallo took the package. "I've got it covered," he assured them.

"I wouldn't trust it with anyone else but you," Amath said earnestly.

"You can count on me," Diallo confirmed. "If this Moussa guy shows up, I'll make sure he gets it safe and sound."

Amath thanked Diallo sincerely, and with that, he and the siblings quickly disappeared around the corner. Diallo, package tucked under one arm, leaned back against a post, feeling pretty good about himself and the world in general. His opinion of the kids, especially Amath, had completely changed. He now saw Amath as a smart, promising young man who was going places. Diallo felt proud to be able to help out by guarding the package.

The package wasn't very heavy, and Diallo wondered what might be inside. Amath had made it seem pretty important, and the fact that Amath trusted only Diallo with it made him feel special.

As the late afternoon sun warmed him, Detective Diallo, leaning comfortably against the post, let his mind wander. He thought about what the siblings had said about him deserving a promotion. He replayed the sound of Amath calling him "Chief." It was music to his ears. Diallo, who was good at catching quick naps while looking alert, started to feel sleepy. He was an expert at this – appearing wide awake when he was actually sneaking in a quick snooze. The hustle and bustle of the 5 o'clock crowd faded into a distant hum of footsteps and voices as he began to drift off.

Suddenly, a shrill alarm clock sound jolted Diallo from his drowsy state. Startled, he straightened up, blinked rapidly, and spun around, trying to figure out where the noise was coming from.

The alarm kept ringing, setting Diallo's nerves on edge. He looked suspiciously at the people nearby, who were also glancing around in confusion. He looked up, then down at the sidewalk, but the mysterious alarm kept blaring.

Then it hit him—the alarm was coming from the package he was holding under his arm. The crowd around him realized it, too, and people started to chuckle.

"Got yourself a personal wake-up call, Detective?" joked a man nearby, clearly amused.

Feeling utterly embarrassed, Diallo was tempted to drop the package right there. But he held back, instead holding it at arm's length by its string. Then he started to weave his way through the crowd, the alarm clock still ringing away.

"Rise and shine, Detective!" someone in the crowd yelled, causing more laughter.

Diallo quickened his pace down the street, his face turning redder with each step. The alarm clock seemed to get louder and louder, echoing in his ears. People turned to look, laughing and pointing, as little kids began to follow him, drawn by the commotion. And through it all, the alarm clock kept up its shrill song, showing no signs of stopping.

Detective Diallo's walk down the street turned into an unplanned parade. A growing line of kids trailed behind him, excited by the bell's nonstop ringing. Diallo found himself the unwilling star of this impromptu show, not sure what to do. Throwing away the package would mean admitting he'd been tricked; holding onto it only made the onlookers laugh more and the bell ring louder.

He walked faster, almost like he was trying to outrun the sound itself. People on the sidewalk stared at him, looking both amused and confused. The laughter and teasing from the crowd grew louder, and the children's shouts became more persistent.

Amath's words echoed mockingly in Diallo's mind: "Your time will come… You're the one to wake this city up… Your leadership will be recognized…" Frustrated and overwhelmed, Diallo finally lost his cool. With an angry grunt, he threw the still-ringing package into a nearby alley.

Unfortunately, his throw hit a uniformed street cleaner who was just stepping out of the alley. The package smacked him right in the chest, knocking him down in surprise. Annoyed, the cleaner tossed it back at Diallo. This only made the crowd laugh even harder. The package landed in the street, the bell still jingling merrily. One of the kids scooped it up and chased after Diallo, innocently trying to give it back to him.

Diallo couldn't shake off his unwanted followers until he reached the police station. Only then did the crowd finally scatter, the alarm clock having run out of battery at last. Inside the station, Diallo wiped his forehead with a handkerchief, his face as red as a tomato and his temper boiling. In his mind, he declared war on all of Zinguichou's kids, especially the high schoolers. Amath's gang was at the top of his list, with Amath himself earning the number one spot in Diallo's personal bad books.

Meanwhile, Amath and his friends had watched the whole hilarious scene from a safe spot. As they headed to the Diouf house, they could barely walk straight because they were laughing so hard. Every few steps, someone would remember Diallo's crazy chase, setting off another round of giggles that left them gasping for air.

"Did you see his face?" Bouma wheezed, holding his sides.

"I thought he was going to pop!" Adama added, wiping tears from her eyes.

Amath, still chuckling, said, "I can't believe he actually threw the package at that poor street cleaner!"

This sent them into another fit of laughter as they stumbled down the street, their prank having succeeded beyond their wildest dreams.

❖

As they reached the Diouf house, still wiping away tears of laughter, the kids were surprised to see Grandma Diouf rushing down the front steps. Her face was serious, a stark contrast to their giggling mood.

"I just got a call from the police station," she announced, her voice tense.

The laughter died in their throats. Boubou asked, "What's going on?" while the others shared worried looks. Had Detective Diallo somehow reported their prank already?

Grandma Diouf's next words wiped the last traces of smiles from their faces. "It's Toto Panko," she said gravely. "He's broken out of jail."

The kids stood there, stunned. Their silly prank suddenly seemed a million miles away.

"Escaped?" Aya echoed, her eyes wide. "But how?"

"When?" Amath added, his prankster grin replaced by a look of concern.

Grandma Diouf shook her head. "I don't have all the details. But it sounds like it just happened now, and the whole police force is on high alert."

The siblings exchanged worried glances. They all remembered Toto Panko - the counterfeiter they'd helped catch not so long ago. If he was on the loose again...

"We should do something," Boubou said, always ready for action.

"Hold on," Grandma Diouf cautioned. "This is serious business. The police are handling it."

But the wheels were already turning in Amath's head. "Of course, Grandma," he said smoothly. "We'll stay out of trouble. Promise."

As they filed into the house, following Grandma Diouf, the kids shared meaningful looks. They all knew that despite their promise, they'd soon be knee-deep in another adventure. After all, how could they resist a mystery like this?

* * *

CHAPTER FIFTEEN

Full Throttle Pursuit

Boubou and Aya's jaws dropped in unison. "What? How did that happen?" they exclaimed, their eyes as wide as saucers at Grandma's news about Toto Panko's daring escape.

"Just a few minutes ago," Grandma replied, her voice steady but tinged with surprise. "He told the guard he wasn't feeling well and needed the bathroom. Next thing you know, Panko had smashed the window and vanished like a magician's trick!"

Aya's forehead wrinkled in thought. "But where could he go? It's not like he can just waltz out of the city."

"You're right," Grandma nodded. "The police have the roads and trains covered. My guess? He's got some shady friends around here who might help him sneak out. Say, why don't you kids team up with Chief Gaye? Take the motorboat and keep an eye on the bay. You never know what you might spot."

Boubou's face lit up like a firework. "That's genius! Come on gang!"

"I'll take my dad's boat out," Pierre piped up, practically bouncing with excitement.

"Now we're talking!" the others cheered. They were racing down the street in a blink, their footsteps drumming out a beat of adventure.

Pierre teamed up with Bouma and Djily, while Amath, Adama, and the Diouf siblings formed another group.

Boubou led the charge to the harbor, the others hot on his heels, their minds whirling with thoughts of the chase to come.

❖

Their excitement crashed like a wave against rocks when they reached the harbor. The Mystery, their trusty motorboat, had vanished into thin air. Only the dripping ropes swayed sadly in the water as if shrugging at the boat's mysterious disappearance.

"Holy cow, the boat's gone!" Boubou shouted, his voice a mix of shock and frustration.

Aya and the others stared at the empty space, their brains struggling to process this new twist.

"Someone swiped it!" Boubou exclaimed, his eyes darting across the water. "And only Aya and I have the keys."

Amath piped up, "It was definitely here at lunch. I saw it before I went to school with my science fair project."

"Who in the world would take it?" Adama wondered, his forehead wrinkled in confusion.

Aya's eyes lit up with a sudden thought. "What if it's Toto Panko? He might've needed a quick getaway."

Boubou nodded, the same idea hitting him. "That's it! He must've thought a boat was his ticket out of here."

"And maybe he found out where we dock," Aya added. "You know, to get back at us for helping the police catch him."

"He's got to be close," Adama reasoned, squinting at the horizon. "Grandma said he escaped not too long ago."

Boubou, filled with renewed determination, raced to the front of the harbor. His eyes scanned the bay like a human radar. Suddenly, he let out a whoop of triumph. "There! I see the Mystery! I'd know that boat anywhere!"

The others sprinted to join him. Boubou pointed excitedly at a tiny white speck zooming across the water to the east. The bay was almost empty, making the Mystery stick out like a sore thumb as it sped away.

"Quick, let's get Pierre to chase him!" Aya yelled, already on the move. "Come on!"

They dashed to the other side of the harbor, their feet pounding the ground. They found Pierre and the others at his dad's boat slip, looking surprised at their sudden appearance. Pierre was just about to set off, the engine purring softly.

"Toto Panko stole our boat!" Boubou blurted out, breathless. "He's zooming across the bay right now!"

"Toto Panko?" Pierre echoed, his eyebrows shooting up to his hairline.

"Yeah, the guy who just broke out of jail. Aya, show him," Boubou urged.

Aya pointed towards the bay. "There's the boat, getting away."

Pierre caught on instantly. He hopped into his motorboat in one smooth motion. "Jump in, quick! We're going after him."

Boubou and Aya leaped aboard, but Adama and the rest hung back.

"Too many of us might slow it down," Adama said, sounding practical but disappointed. "You guys need to be fast to catch him. We'd only get in the way."

Even though they were itching to join the chase, Adama knew speed trumped numbers right now. The others quickly agreed, deciding to stay behind.

"We'll call Zabrousse village," Adama shouted over the engine's roar. "Maybe they can send out a boat and cut him off!"

His words were nearly drowned out as Pierre expertly maneuvered his motorboat, backing it into open water. He pointed them towards the open bay with a quick spin of the wheel.

"Bet you're wishing the Mystery wasn't faster than my boat right now," Pierre said with a mischievous grin. "This might be trickier than we thought."

He pushed the throttle, and the boat surged forward, slicing through the water and leaving a trail of foamy waves behind them.

❖

Far ahead, the white dot of the stolen Mystery zipped across the bay. Toto Panko wasn't wasting any time. It looked like the police hadn't figured out his escape plan yet, as Pierre's boat was the only one chasing him. It wasn't clear if Panko even knew he was being followed.

"Going full speed ahead," Pierre announced, his hands steady on the wheel as he pushed the boat to its limits.

The motorboat hummed and shook with power, cutting through the water like a knife. The kids could see they were slowly gaining on the Mystery, probably because Toto Panko thought he'd gotten away clean and wasn't pushing his stolen boat as hard.

"If we can sneak up on him before he notices us, we might just catch him," Aya said, her eyes glued to the distant boat.

"Keep dreaming," Pierre replied with a grin. "He's bound to look back sooner or later."

Boubou found a pair of binoculars on a seat and peered through them. Suddenly, the Mystery and its driver seemed much closer. Through the lenses, Boubou could clearly see the man at the wheel.

It was definitely Toto Panko.

As Boubou watched, Panko glanced back, and his face twisted in shock. He'd spotted them.

Boubou saw Panko lean into the throttle, and the Mystery shot forward. Its front sliced through the water more fiercely, sending spray flying into the air. The boat started pulling away, widening the gap.

"He's seen us," Boubou said, lowering the binoculars.

"We're not giving up that easy," Pierre declared, his eyes locked on the escaping boat.

With a hint of bravado, Pierre added, "We'll chase him all the way to the ocean if we have to!"

Aya's face suddenly lit up. "The gas! That's our secret weapon! I checked the Mystery's tank at noon, and it was almost empty. He can't have much fuel left."

"Brilliant!" Pierre exclaimed, new energy in his voice. "The Mystery might be faster, but we've got more gas. My tank's full, plus we've got extra. We'll stay on his tail until he has to stop."

Despite the Mystery's potential fuel problem, it showed no signs of slowing down. The boat zoomed ahead in the bay, steadily increasing its lead. Focused and determined, Pierre kept his eyes on the distant white blur of the Mystery.

"Any idea where he's heading?" Boubou wondered, watching the chase intently.

"Probably sticking to the coast," Pierre guessed. "I bet he'll dash out of the bay and zoom up the coast as far as he can, then ditch the boat."

Aya said, "That sounds like his plan, but he won't get far. The Mystery's gas won't last long enough to get out of the bay."

Toto Panko wasn't heading for Zabrousse village. Instead, he was steering toward the other side of the bay, toward the Cazamoun River's mouth.

"He might be thinking of taking the river route," Boubou suggested thoughtfully.

Pierre shook his head. "Bad move if he does. He'd end up right in the middle of the falls and rapids near the old power plant."

"Oh, right," Boubou said, remembering those natural obstacles.

As the Mystery neared the river's mouth, it started to slow down.

"Yes!" Aya cheered. "She's running out of gas!"

Boubou crossed his fingers. "Let's hope so. Panko must be feeling pretty stuck right about now."

But just when their hopes were high, the Mystery seemed to pick up speed again.

"Oh, come on!" Aya groaned. "Just when we thought we had him."

Then, a sputtering sound echoed across the water from the Mystery's direction.

"That's the sound of an empty gas tank," Boubou said with a grin. "I can't wait for him to come to a complete stop."

"You and me both," Pierre agreed, his eyes glued to the slowing boat.

Bit by bit, the Mystery slowed to a crawl.

Boubou grabbed the binoculars again, eager to see what was happening on the distant boat.

Through the lenses, he watched Toto Panko desperately fiddling with the motor, trying to figure out what was wrong. Panko kept looking back nervously, his face a picture of worry.

"He knows he's trapped," Boubou said quietly.

They closed in on the Mystery, which was now barely moving, just bobbing on the waves. In a last attempt to escape, Panko grabbed an emergency paddle from the boat and started rowing towards the shore, his movements frantic but useless.

But it was too late. Pierre's motorboat was right behind him, and the Mystery's engine had completely given up.

As they pulled up next to him, Panko threw the paddle aside, admitting defeat without a word. He slumped in the boat, avoiding their eyes.

"Tough break, Panko!" Boubou called out. "Looks like you're coming back with us."

Panko grumbled, "Would've been fine if the darn gas hadn't run out."

Aya said with a hint of sarcasm, "Well, we were more interested in getting our boat back than catching you. Are you going to come quietly?"

Panko just shrugged, accepting his fate.

"Guess I don't have much choice," Panko sighed. "And no, I don't have any weapons. If I did, you bet I'd put up a fight."

"Glad to hear it," Pierre replied lightly. He skillfully brought his boat close to the Mystery, letting Boubou and Aya hop back onto their reclaimed vessel.

Panko didn't cause any trouble. They tied his wrists with a strong rope from the stern, and he sat down, looking thoughtful.

"I'll get out again," he told them, a bit of defiance in his voice. "If I can't break out myself, my friends will make sure I'm free."

Boubou, now thinking practically, turned to Pierre. "So, how do we get back?"

Panko chuckled. "That's your problem, not mine. You're out of gas, remember?"

Pierre pulled out a can of gasoline from his boat without missing a beat. "Always good to be prepared," he said, handing it over.

Panko went quiet, out of tricks and options. The Diouf siblings filled the Mystery's tank with the extra gas, and soon, its engine roared back to life.

Together, the two boats turned around and headed back to Zinguichou, side by side, as the sun started to set.

CHAPTER SIXTEEN

Elaborating A Plan

After the heart-pounding chase and capture of Toto Panko, Boubou and Aya Diouf, along with their friend Pierre Leroy, found themselves swimming in a sea of well-deserved praise. Even Chief Gaye, who usually kept compliments locked away tighter than a miser's wallet, let one slip. He admitted their quick thinking had led to a clever capture. Maybe his sudden generosity came from knowing that if Toto Panko had vanished into thin air, the Chief would've been in hot water with the locals, especially since his own Deputy, Detective Diallo, had messed things up royally.

Lucky for Chief Gaye, all the excitement about catching Toto Panko made people forget about the jail mishap. He breathed a huge sigh of relief, knowing that if the slippery criminal had stayed on the loose, folks would've been quick to blame the police for every missing cookie in town.

The Diouf siblings' role in all this reminded everyone of their past adventures. People couldn't stop talking about how the kids solved the spooky Lighthouse mystery and cracked the case of the fisherman's house smugglers. You'd often hear someone in the crowd say with a grin, "Those kids have their father's detective genes, alright. Mark my words; they'll be solving crimes with the best of 'em someday!"

For Boubou and Aya, nothing felt better than hearing people recognize their growing detective skills. It was like carrying on their famous father's legacy. Their recent wins, like nabbing Toto Panko, were even starting to win over Grandma Diouf. She'd always been a bit nervous about their detective dreams, but now she was beginning to see that their desire to become real detectives wasn't just kid stuff – it was the real deal.

Aya couldn't help but quip, "Hey Boubou, maybe we should start charging for autographs. We could make enough to buy Grandma a lifetime supply of her favorite tea!"

Boubou rolled his eyes but couldn't hide his grin. "Sure, and maybe Chief Gaye will start a comedy club while he's at it."

While Toto Panko was now behind bars, counterfeit money continued to plague the streets of Zinguichou and Zabrousse village. It seemed like every other day, someone was walking into the police station or a bank with a bewildered look on their face, holding a fake note that had fooled them. The counterfeiters were still at large, and their handiwork was turning up everywhere.

Take the local garage owner, for example. He had unknowingly traded a crisp $100 bill for some gas and oil to a customer who zoomed in and out faster than a hiccup. Or consider the mess at the ferry ticket office. They'd accepted a fake $50 bill for a ticket. They did not realize their mistake until Papa Seck, the ticket seller, counted the day's take. The weirdest part? The ticket, which only cost $8, was tracked down by its number, only to discover it never even made it onto the ferry.

Aya couldn't resist a joke. "Looks like our mystery customer bought a ticket to nowhere."

The city was abuzz with such stories. Everyone was on high alert, trying to spot these fake notes. But here's the kicker – the forgeries were so convincing, and the stories spun by those trying to pass them off so believable that even the most cautious folks found themselves duped. It was clear that despite Toto Panko's capture, the counterfeiters were still running a rampant game in town.

The circulation of these counterfeit notes wasn't confined to the shady corners of Zinguichou; even the most reputable citizens were unwittingly handing them over to local merchants. These upstanding individuals, taken aback upon discovering the notes' falsity, would explain that they had received them in all innocence from others just as trustworthy. Tracing the origin of these fraudulent notes was like trying to catch a shadow; they had slipped through countless unsuspecting hands, their deceit unnoticed.

Boubou and Aya couldn't stop talking about the mystery of the fake money. They often chatted about it with their grandmother, who decided it was time for something special - a way to connect with their late father's spirit. The kids watched in wonder as Grandma Diouf got ready for what she called a "divination ritual."

She spread out a colorful mat and carefully placed small shells in a pattern. The room filled with the sweet smell of incense, making everything feel magical and exciting.

Grandma sat cross-legged on the floor, her hands hovering over a basket of shells. With a quick flick of her wrist, she tossed the shells, scattering them across the mat with soft clicking sounds. Her eyes, sharp as hawk's, followed every move. As the shells settled, they formed a pattern that looked random to Boubou and Aya but seemed to mean a lot to Grandma.

She studied the shells like a secret map, each telling its own story. To Grandma, this wasn't just a bunch of shells—it was a message from the spirit world, which she could read as easily as a favorite book.

As Grandma began to speak, her voice changed, becoming softer and distant. It was as if their father was speaking through her. It gave Boubou and Aya goosebumps!

"Keep this to yourselves," Grandma warned in a voice that didn't quite sound like her own, "but your father says the police task force found clues that the fake money might be coming from near Zabrousse village."

Aya leaned in, her detective instincts tingling. "Do they know exactly where, Dad?" she asked, excited and a little spooked.

"They think it's hidden deep in the woods, maybe in an old farmhouse," Grandma answered, sounding like their dad. "The land across the bay is wild and full of places to hide. It's perfect for the bad guys making the fake money."

Through Grandma, their father's spirit told them about different places the police were watching. But even with all their searching, they hadn't found any real proof yet.

"Most of the fake money is showing up right here, around Zinguichou and Zabrousse," Grandma continued, still channeling their dad's voice. "The place where they're actually printing the money might be somewhere in the middle of all this."

As the ritual ended, Boubou and Aya quietly stood up. They knew Grandma needed to prepare for grocery shopping and dinner prep. As they left, their minds were buzzing with all this new information. What would their next move be in solving the mystery of the fake money makers?

Aya's eyes sparkled with determination as she whispered to Boubou, "This could be the breakthrough we've been waiting for."

Boubou grinned back, "Yeah, but remember - this is our secret mission. No blabbing to the whole school this time!"

❖

Aya lounged in their dad's old study chair, feeling like a real detective. "This fake money case could be our big break, Boubou," she said, her eyes twinkling with excitement. "The whole town's talking about it. Imagine if we solved it!"

Boubou, always practical, raised an eyebrow. "There are better detectives than us working on this," he reminded her.

"Yeah, and they're totally stuck," Aya shot back.

"True," Boubou admitted. "If only we could get Toto Panko to talk. He might give us a clue."

Aya shook her head. "He's not saying a word. Besides, I don't think he knows much about where the fake money's coming from. He's probably just a small part of their plan to spread the phony cash around."

Boubou nodded thoughtfully. "You might be right. Like that guy at the garage or the ferry ticket office – they probably had no idea they were using fake money. It's a tricky business."

Aya leaned forward, her face serious. "I've been thinking about where this fake money keeps showing up. It's mostly here in Zinguichou. Doesn't that seem weird to you?"

"Yeah, it's like the bad guys are focusing on our town," Boubou agreed.

"Exactly!" Aya exclaimed. "If the fake money is mostly found here, maybe the source is nearby. And here's my crazy idea - what if they're hiding somewhere nobody would expect?"

Boubou's eyes widened. "Like where?"

"Well," Aya paused dramatically, "what if they're right under our noses? Maybe in a basement downtown. Somewhere so obvious that no one would think to look."

Boubou's jaw dropped. "That's... actually pretty smart. They could be working right next door, and we'd never know!"

Aya nodded excitedly. "And I can't shake this feeling, Boubou. I keep thinking about that old power plant. Remember how weird they were about not letting me dry my clothes there? And then that whole thing with the money..."

Boubou's brow furrowed. "Yeah, that guy was really pushy about giving us a reward. And his friend acted strange when he took the money back."

"Exactly!" Aya exclaimed. "What if they switched the fake money for real money so we wouldn't get suspicious?"

Boubou's eyes lit up. "Whoa, Aya. You might be onto something big. What if the old power plant is actually where they're making the fake money? It's the perfect cover!"

"That's what I'm saying!" Aya replied. "They claim they're making some new battery, but it doesn't add up."

"And those guys didn't exactly look like scientists," Boubou chuckled.

"But how are we going to find out more?" Boubou wondered. "They've got that place locked up tight."

Aya grinned. "Remember Kirabo? The kid we saved? I bet he could tell us what's really going on in there."

Boubou's eyes sparkled. "Brilliant! If Kirabo tells us even a little bit about their story, we can figure out if it's true or not."

"And if those guys are up to no good, Kirabo might be dying to tell someone," Boubou added.

Aya nodded. "Exactly. We need to be careful, though. We don't want to cause trouble if we're wrong."

"How about we bike up there tomorrow morning?" Aya suggested. "Maybe we can talk to Kirabo."

"I'm in," Boubou declared. "It's Saturday, so even if they see us, we'll just look like kids out for a ride."

With their plan set, the Diouf siblings felt like real detectives. They were determined to solve the mystery of the old power plant and the fake money. Talking to Kirabo seemed like their best shot at cracking the case. After all, they had saved his life – surely he'd want to help them out!

As they prepared for bed, Aya couldn't resist one last joke. "Hey, Boubou, if this detective thing doesn't work out, maybe we can start our own fake money business. We could call it 'Diouf Dollars: So Real, Even We Can't Tell the Difference!'"

Boubou groaned but couldn't hide his smile. "Very funny, Aya. Let's stick to solving mysteries, not creating them!"

CHAPTER SEVENTEEN

Kirabo's Revelation

Boubou and Aya Diouf, brother and sister detective extraordinaire, were up with the sun, ready for their next big adventure. Their destination? The creepy old power plant by the Cazamoun River. They pedaled their bikes along the shore road, tires humming like excited bees, before turning onto a secret path that wound its way to the abandoned building.

As the river came into view, sparkling like a million diamonds, they hid their bikes under some leafy trees. "Time for some sneaky-sneaky," Aya whispered, wiggling her eyebrows.

Boubou grinned, holding up their fishing poles. "Yep, and we're going to catch some fish while we're at it!"

"Ooh, clever!" Aya giggled. "We can hang around the power plant without looking suspicious. Plus, remember how the fish near the old plant were always super tasty?"

Boubou nodded, his eyes twinkling with mischief. "Two birds, one stone, sis!"

They crept through the woods, feeling like spies on a top-secret mission. When they reached the river, they cast their lines, watching the colorful bobbers dance on the water. Inch by inch, they made their way downstream, moving as quietly as cats stalking mice.

By the time the power plant loomed into view, looking like a giant metal monster, their bucket was home to three silvery fish. Aya peeked inside, whispering dramatically, "Sorry, fishy friends. Your sacrifice won't be in vain!"

❖

The rusty old power plant creaked and groaned, its giant wheel turning lazily in the river. Inside, machines hummed softly, creating a strange lullaby. By the water's edge, a lone figure stood motionless.

"Hey, isn't that Kirabo?" Aya whispered, her eyes wide with excitement.

Boubou squinted and nodded. "Yep, that's him alright. Looks like he's trying to fish."

Kirabo stood on the riverbank, holding a fishing rod. But he didn't look too thrilled about it. His eyes were dull as he watched the red and white bobber dance on the water's surface.

Boubou and Aya walked down to join him. When Kirabo spotted them, his face lit up like a Christmas tree.

"Hey guys!" he called out, sounding a bit shy.

"Hi Kirabo," they answered together. "Catch anything good?"

"Not even a minnow," Kirabo sighed, shrugging his shoulders. "To be honest, I'm not really into fishing."

"That's weird," Boubou said. "This spot's usually crawling with fish."

Kirabo shrugged again. "Maybe. I mean, I've caught some before. But when it's all you do day after day, it gets pretty boring, you know?"

Aya leaned in, curious. "Is fishing really all you do around here?"

"Pretty much," Kirabo replied, sounding lonelier than a penguin in the desert. "Living at this old power plant isn't exactly a non-stop party."

"Why don't you go into town sometimes?" Boubou suggested.

Kirabo's face fell. "I wish. But Uncle Dogo won't let me."

As they talked, Kirabo seemed to perk up. He plopped down on the riverbank, completely forgetting about his fishing rod. It was like he was soaking up every second of conversation like a sponge.

"Do you guys go to school?" he asked, his voice full of longing.

The Diouf siblings nodded.

"Like, every single day?"

"Yep, every day except weekends," they replied.

Kirabo's gaze drifted off, like he was imagining a whole different life. "Man, I wish I could go to school. You guys are so lucky."

Aya and Boubou looked at each other, their eyes wide with shock. They'd never met anyone who didn't go to school, let alone someone who thought it was something to be jealous of. It was like Kirabo had just told them he'd never eaten food or breathed air.

"Wait," Boubou said slowly, trying to wrap his head around the idea. "You mean you've never been to school? Ever?"

Kirabo shook his head. "Nope. Never."

Aya's mouth fell open. "But... but how do you learn stuff? Where do you meet other kids?"

"I don't," Kirabo shrugged, looking a bit sad. "Uncle Dogo teaches me some things, but mostly I'm on my own."

The Diouf siblings were stunned into silence. All their complaints about early mornings, tough teachers, and mountains of homework suddenly seemed ridiculous. They'd always taken school for granted, but now they were seeing it through Kirabo's eyes - as an amazing opportunity they were lucky to have.

"Wow," Boubou finally managed to say. "I guess we are pretty lucky. Even if it doesn't always feel that way."

Aya nodded, still looking dazed. "Yeah, I never thought I'd say this, but... school is actually kind of awesome when you think about it."

Kirabo nodded eagerly. "It must be! Are there lots of other kids there?"

"Oh yeah, tons," Aya replied, her voice filled with new appreciation.

As they continued talking, Aya and Boubou couldn't shake the feeling that their world had just gotten a whole lot bigger - and a whole lot more complicated. Meeting Kirabo was like opening a door to a reality they never knew existed, and they weren't sure they liked what they saw on the other side.

Kirabo let out a wistful sigh. "Wow, that must be amazing. But Uncle Dogo, he's super strict about me going anywhere."

Boubou, curious, asked, "Where are you from originally?"

"Batou," Kirabo answered. "But I never really got to know anyone there either. Uncle Dogo always kept me on a short leash. He says someday we'll be rich, and then I can have all the friends I want."

Aya's eyebrows shot up. "What does your uncle do, exactly?"

"He runs the power plant," Kirabo answered, looking a bit confused by the question.

"But what does he make here?" Boubou wondered. "Some kind of super-battery or something?"

"Honestly, I have no clue," Kirabo shrugged. "Uncle Dogo doesn't tell me anything about his work."

"Did he bring in any new equipment when you guys moved in?" Boubou asked.

"Yeah, a bunch of new machines arrived when we first got here. They're all locked up in a room at the back."

Aya tried to sound casual. "What do they look like?"

Kirabo shrugged again. "No idea. I've never seen them. They're in this special room, and the door's always locked. Uncle Dogo blew his top once when he caught me hanging around near it."

"Have you ever seen any of these super-batteries they're supposed to be making?" Boubou pressed.

Kirabo shook his head. "Nope, never seen anything like that."

"Do they ship stuff out?" Boubou asked.

Kirabo hesitated for a moment, like he was trying to decide what to say.

"Mr. Mako sometimes goes to town with some packages, but they're not very big," he finally said.

"Is Mr. Mako related to you?" Aya asked.

"No, he's not. I'd never met him or the other guy until Uncle Dogo brought me here," Kirabo explained.

Boubou's face grew serious. "Is Dogo really your uncle?"

"Yeah, he is. He's been taking care of me for about a year now since my dad died."

"Is he... is he nice to you?" Boubou asked gently.

Kirabo's face clouded over. "Sometimes. But he's super strict about me not going to school or having friends. And he gets really mad if I don't do exactly what he says."

Aya, trying to lighten the mood, asked, "What did he do back in Batou? Did he make batteries there too?"

Kirabo couldn't help but laugh. "In Batou? He didn't do much of anything. He'd go out at night and leave me alone. Sometimes, he wouldn't come back until the sun was almost up. He said he was working at a factory. But then these weird guys would visit him, and they'd talk for hours."

Boubou, still curious, asked, "So he never really talked to you about this super-battery business?"

"Not a word," Kirabo confirmed.

"How long are you planning to stay here?" Aya inquired.

Kirabo shrugged. "Uncle Dogo said maybe another month. But he always has a suitcase packed, like we might leave any second."

The Diouf siblings exchanged a look. It was becoming pretty clear that Uncle Dogo might not be the brilliant scientist they'd thought he was.

Kirabo's eyes were full of dreams. "I just wish we were rich already. I'd love to get out of here, go to school, maybe even move to your town, and go to school with you guys. But that's probably just a pipe dream."

Boubou leaned in. "Your uncle seems pretty sure about getting rich, huh?"

"Yeah, he's always saying that we'll be rolling in cash soon, and then I can have all the friends I want," Kirabo replied, sounding like he didn't really believe it.

"He must be betting everything on this super-battery thing," Boubou mused.

"I guess so," Kirabo agreed, though he didn't sound convinced.

Aya, looking puzzled, asked, "Don't batteries need stuff like copper and charcoal? Has your uncle ever bought any metal or equipment from people around here?"

Kirabo shook his head. "Nope, never. Some farmers have come by to ask, but he always sends them away."

"So what's he using to make these super-batteries?" Boubou wondered out loud.

"I really don't know anything about it," Kirabo admitted with a shrug. "Uncle Dogo keeps all his work stuff top secret. He never lets me anywhere near the workroom."

It was clear that was all Kirabo knew about Uncle Dogo's mysterious business. But he didn't seem to mind the questions; it was obvious he was starved for conversation and was thrilled to have someone to talk to. The more the Diouf siblings learned about life at the old power plant, the more suspicious they became of Uncle Dogo and his secretive operation.

Boubou, changing the subject, asked, "Does your uncle have you do any chores around here?"

"Just little stuff like chopping wood sometimes and getting water from the spring. But really, there's not much to do. It gets super boring. I wish I had more to keep me busy. Most of the time, I just fish, swim, and lie around like a lazy cat."

"Doesn't your uncle ever let you help out in the power plant?"

Kirabo rolled his eyes. "No way. My uncle never lets me anywhere near the workroom. I've asked a million times, but they act like I'm trying to break into Fort Knox or something."

"Workroom? They don't use the rest of the power plant?" Aya asked, her curiosity piqued.

Kirabo leaned in like he was sharing a big secret. "It's just this one room where they keep all the fancy new machines. The rest of the place? It's like a ghost town, all dusty and abandoned."

Suddenly, a booming voice interrupted their chat. They all turned to look at the power plant. There stood Uncle Dogo in the doorway, looking madder than a wet hen.

"Kirabo!" he yelled, his voice echoing across the river.

Kirabo's reply was barely a whisper. "Yeah?"

"Get over here, now!" Uncle Dogo's voice could have woken the dead. He started stomping down the hill towards them.

"Uh-oh, I'm in for it now," Kirabo mumbled, looking worried. "Uncle Dogo's gonna be mad that I was talking to you guys."

And boy, was he right. Uncle Dogo marched up to them, grumbling like an angry bear.

"Kirabo, back to the power plant, pronto!" he barked, giving Kirabo a little tap on the head. "How many times do I have to tell you? Don't talk to strangers. You're always running your mouth. Get back inside and stay put."

Kirabo tried to defend himself. "But we were just talking—"

Uncle Dogo cut him off with a look that could have frozen lava.

Kirabo gave Aya and Boubou a helpless look, then trudged back up the hill towards the power plant. Uncle Dogo turned to the siblings, eyeing them like they were a pair of troublemaking raccoons.

"What are you two doing here, loitering around?" he snapped.

"We're not loitering. We've been fishing down by the river," Boubou replied coolly. "And honestly, it's none of your business."

Uncle Dogo's face turned as red as a tomato. "I'll make it my business!" He glared at them. "You two better scram. We don't need you hanging around here."

"But the river's for everyone," Aya pointed out calmly.

"Stay away from this power plant, or you'll be sorry. And what was that chatterbox Kirabo yakking about with you?" Uncle Dogo demanded.

"Just talking," Boubou answered vaguely.

"Well, no more chatting with him. I don't want Kirabo gabbing with every random kid who happens to stroll by. It'd be best if you two steered clear from here on out."

With that, Uncle Dogo stomped back up the hill to the power plant, still grumbling to himself. The Diouf siblings, unfazed by his outburst but sensing they'd stumbled onto something big, slowly started walking down the riverbank, moving away from the old power plant and its grumpy guardian.

As they walked, Aya turned to Boubou with a mischievous grin. "Well, that was about as subtle as a fireworks show in a library. What do you think Uncle Grumpy Pants is really up to in there?"

Boubou stroked his chin thoughtfully. "I don't know, but I bet it's not making super-batteries. Maybe he's trying to invent a machine that turns broccoli into ice cream."

Aya laughed. "Or a device that makes homework disappear!"

They both chuckled, but their laughter faded as they thought about poor Kirabo, trapped in that creepy old power plant with his mysterious uncle.

"We've got to help him somehow," Aya said softly.

Boubou nodded, his face serious. "Yeah, but how? Uncle Dogo's not exactly the friendly neighborhood type."

"We'll figure something out," Aya said, determination shining in her eyes. "After all, we're the Diouf siblings. Solving mysteries and helping friends is what we do best!"

And with that, they continued down the riverbank, their minds buzzing with plans and possibilities. Little did they know, their biggest adventure yet was just beginning.

$$* \quad * \quad *$$

CHAPTER EIGHTEEN

The Clandestine Exchange

BOUBOU PEDALED HARDER, THE WIND WHIPPING THROUGH his hair as he and Aya zoomed back to Zinguichou. "So, what do you think, Aya?"

Aya, riding beside him, rolled her eyes. "Honestly? This whole 'Uncle Dogo the Scientist' story smells fishier than last week's catch. Since when do scientists treat batteries like they're guarding the secret recipe for eternal youth?"

Boubou snorted. "Right? And all that secrecy! Not even letting Kirabo peek inside the workroom? It's weirder than a horizontal striped zebra."

"Weird is an understatement," Aya grinned, her eyes sparkling with mischief. "Uncle Dogo's about as welcoming as a cactus at a balloon festival."

"Poor Kirabo," Boubou's voice softened. "Stuck with that bunch of oddballs. I'm surprised he hasn't vanished into thin air yet."

Aya's face turned thoughtful. "He probably feels trapped. He's a good kid in a sticky situation."

"Yeah," Boubou nodded. "We didn't get much info, but it's enough to know something's up in that old power plant."

"I'd trade my favorite goggles for a peek at that secret room Kirabo mentioned," Aya said, wiggling her eyebrows.

Boubou groaned. "Too bad Uncle Dogo spotted us. If we show up again, he'll be watching us like a leopard eyeing its prey."

"Maybe we should tell Grandma and talk to Dad?" Aya suggested.

But Boubou shook his head, determination etched on his face. "Nah, we should keep digging on our own. We need solid proof, not just hunches and guesses."

"You're right," Aya agreed, smacking her forehead. "We can't always run to Dad. Time to put on our detective hats and do some real sleuthing!"

As they pedaled toward Zinguichou, Boubou and Aya's minds raced with theories about the mystery at the power plant. They knew the trio's actions screamed "Not normal science stuff!" But they also realized that poking their noses too far could land them in hot water.

"Let's lay low for now, but keep our eyes peeled," Boubou said finally, his voice a mix of caution and excitement. "If these guys are up to something shady, they'll mess up eventually. And when they do—" he grinned at Aya, "—we'll be ready to crack this case wide open!"

Back home, Boubou and Aya zipped straight to their dad's study. Surrounded by towering bookshelves, they lost themselves in reading for a while, a quiet break from their earlier escapades.

Soon enough, their stomachs started grumbling. "Time for a snack attack!" Aya declared. They raided the kitchen, emerging with an armful of treats. Their giggles bounced off the walls as they munched away.

Feeling refreshed after snacks and quick showers, they decided to venture out into the lazy Saturday afternoon.

The city streets were as quiet as a mouse in a library. "Wow, it's like everyone's taking a group nap," Boubou said, stifling a yawn. "Maybe we should've hung out in the countryside a bit longer."

Aya's eyes suddenly lit up with an idea. "Hey, why don't we take the motorboat out for a spin? That'll wake us up!"

Boubou's face broke into a huge grin. "Now you're talking! Let's go!"

And just like that, they were off again, ready to trade the sleepy streets for some watery adventures. As they raced towards the docks, Aya couldn't help but wonder what exciting - or maybe even mysterious - things they might discover out on the water.

❖

As they hopped on their bikes, the whistle of the afternoon express train cut through the air. Suddenly, Aya felt a weird, tingly sensation wash over her. It was like warm, magical syrup was flowing through her veins, bringing with it fuzzy pictures and feelings that somehow connected her to her dad's spirit. Without really knowing why, she found herself pedaling towards the train station. Boubou, seeing the serious look on his sister's face, followed without a word.

This wasn't the first time Aya had experienced these strange visions. They'd started back when they were solving the case of the diamond smugglers. During one of Grandma's special sessions, Aya had felt an overwhelming presence, as if their dad was right there in the room, speaking through Grandma. It filled Aya with a warm, fuzzy feeling of love and a deep connection to her dad's memory.

Now those visions were coming back, reminding Aya of how Grandma first discovered her own gift for seeing things others couldn't. Grandma often told them how it started with faint whispers and messages only she could hear. Aya always loved watching her grandmother's sessions, and she was amazed by all the different people who came to their house. Each visitor had their own secrets and stories, hoping Grandma could give them answers or even work miracles.

Sometimes, when school felt super boring, Aya would sneak home early and peek through the window, wondering what Grandma saw in her clients. Aya never quite felt brave enough to try any of this mystical stuff herself - her practical side always held her back. But she couldn't help being fascinated by the unknown, the shiny cowrie shells Grandma used, and all the mysteries of the world that seemed just out of reach.

As they neared the train station, Aya's heart raced with excitement and a little bit of fear. What would these visions show her this time? And was she ready to embrace this part of herself that seemed to connect her to something bigger than she could understand?

Boubou and Aya reached the train station just as the express train glided to a stop. They stood there, watching the passengers get on and off, admiring the cool, calm engineer in the cab and the smart-looking conductor in his crisp uniform. Their eyes roamed over the busy platform, taking in all the people rushing around, each caught up in their own journey.

Suddenly, Boubou nudged Aya. "Look," he whispered urgently. "Isn't that Mako over there?"

Aya followed his gaze. Near one of the train cars stood a man in a low-pulled cap. His posture and movement were unmistakable—it was definitely Mako, one of Uncle Dogo's buddies from the old power plant.

What really caught their attention was the bulky paper package Mako was hugging like it was made of gold. He kept glancing around nervously as if worried someone might be watching him.

Realizing they needed to be sneaky, Boubou and Aya quickly ducked behind a nearby pillar. From their hiding spot, they watched closely, their minds buzzing with questions about what Mako was up to and what could be in that mysterious package.

Mako seemed jumpy as he lingered near the train car, his eyes darting around. It was clear he was waiting for someone.

The moment got even more intense when the conductor called out, "All aboard!" Almost instantly, a tall man with a thin face and a neat black mustache stepped out of the train car. He moved quickly, almost like he was trying not to be noticed. He and Mako did a super quick nod thing, leaned in to whisper something, and then - whoosh! - the tall guy snatched the package from Mako and disappeared back onto the train.

Mako looked so relieved once the package was gone, like a huge weight had been lifted off his shoulders. With a casual shrug, he spun around and strolled away, vanishing into the crowd just as the train started to chug away.

The whole thing happened so fast that nobody else on the platform even seemed to notice. To any other person, it might have looked like nothing special. But to Boubou and Aya, this quick handoff was super suspicious, especially given the weird stuff going on at the abandoned power plant.

Aya looked at Boubou, her eyes wide with curiosity and worry. "What do you think that was all about?"

"Looks like Mako was passing along a 'sample' of their so-called new super battery," Boubou replied, making air quotes.

"But he was acting so secretive," Aya pointed out.

"Yeah, way too cloak-and-dagger for batteries," Boubou agreed. "Did you notice how they waited until the last second before the train left?"

"Definitely not how you'd handle normal batteries," Aya mused.

"I don't think it's batteries at all," Boubou said, shaking his head. "It's obvious that Mako and his gang are communicating with someone here in the city. Remember what Kirabo told us? Mako often comes to Zinguichou carrying a package just like that one. It's got to be part of whatever they're up to."

Aya nodded in agreement. "Well, we've got another piece of the puzzle now. This is getting more interesting by the minute."

"Give them enough time, and they'll trip themselves up," Boubou said confidently. "I bet anything that what's in that package isn't batteries, but fake money. Mako has 'sneaky' written all over him, and his buddy on the train didn't exactly look trustworthy either. My guess? They're using the old power plant as a cover for printing counterfeit bills. Then, they hand it off to someone on the train, who spreads it around in another city."

Aya nodded, her expression thoughtful. "You're probably right. Mako definitely looked like he was carrying something way more important than batteries when he handed over that package. He was acting super sketchy."

"Smart thinking, heading to the station," Boubou remarked. "It's almost like you knew this was going to happen! How did you guess?"

Aya smiled mysteriously. "I didn't know for sure. It was just a feeling, like a hunch. You know, ever since we started getting involved in these mysteries, I've been feeling these instincts more strongly. It's like I can sense when something's about to happen. Today, when I heard the train, something just clicked in my brain, telling me to come here. It's weird, but it's been happening more and more lately."

Boubou looked at her with a mix of admiration and curiosity. "That's incredible, Aya. It's like you've got a built-in mystery radar or something."

With these thoughts spinning in their heads, the siblings headed back down the street, still talking about everything they'd discovered. They decided to spend the rest of the afternoon in Zinguichou, doing what they loved best: solving mysteries aboard their beloved boat, the Mystery.

For now, they chose to put the power plant puzzle on the back burner, confident in Boubou's belief that the counterfeiters, if that's what they were, would eventually reveal their own guilt through some slip-up or mistake. And when they did, Boubou and Aya would be ready to crack the case wide open!

❖

When Boubou and Aya got home for dinner, they decided to keep their discoveries a secret. But to their surprise, Grandma Diouf brought up something interesting during the meal. "I got a call from the government investigators this afternoon," she said casually. "They were asking if you two had found out anything new since Toto Panko was caught."

Aya's eyes sparkled with excitement. "Do you think they want us to help with their investigation?" she asked hopefully.

"The authorities believe that over $10,000 in fake money has been passed around in just the last few days," Grandma revealed, her voice serious.

"Whoa," Aya gasped. "This is way bigger than we thought!"

Boubou, always trying to connect the dots, asked, "What about Toto Panko? Has he said anything?"

Grandma shook her head. "Funny you should ask. I wondered the same thing. They told me they haven't been able to get him to say a single word." She sounded as frustrated as the investigators.

Boubou thought for a moment. "I'm starting to think Toto Panko might not know who the big bosses are. He was probably just used to spreading the fake money around."

"The authorities did say they'd like you two to keep an eye out for any more clues," Grandma Diouf added.

Boubou nodded. "Makes sense. Catching these counterfeiters would really help them out." He sounded determined.

"And don't forget, there's a big reward too!" Aya said excitedly.

Grandma Diouf looked at them, worried but understanding. "I guess they know I can't really stop you kids from investigating. They did say, though, that if you're going to help, be careful and don't do anything dangerous." Her tone was firm, showing how serious this was.

Boubou and Aya glanced at each other, thinking about what Grandma said. They both wondered what she'd feel if she knew how much they were already involved. The clues they'd found so far really pointed to the old power plant by the Cazamoun River being part of the counterfeiting operation. But they kept quiet about this, knowing they needed to be careful and how important this case was.

What Boubou and Aya didn't know was that Grandma had kept part of her phone call with the government investigator secret, too. The investigator had actually praised their past successes. "I know they've shown real talent in solving cases before. If they crack this one and give us solid evidence," he'd said with a little laugh, "we'll have to admit they've got a real gift for detective work."

"Oh, please don't encourage them too much," Grandma Diouf had quickly said, trying to protect them.

But the investigator wasn't worried. "Come on, Ma'am. If they're drawn to detective work and they're good at it, you can't really stop them. It's like trying to stop water from flowing downhill. I knew their father well. He had a sharp mind for this kind of thing, and the apple doesn't fall far from the tree. They've already proven themselves with the Lighthouse diamond theft and the blood diamond smugglers' ring."

Even though she was worried, Grandma Diouf couldn't help feeling proud. "And I have a strong feeling they'll make a breakthrough in this case, too," she'd said.

As dinner wrapped up, Boubou and Aya were bursting with excitement, ready to dive deeper into their investigation. They knew they had to be careful, but the thrill of the mystery and the chance to help catch real criminals was just too exciting to ignore.

CHAPTER NINETEEN

A Rug, A Ruse, And Ruin

TWO DAYS AFTER WHAT SEEMED LIKE JUST ANOTHER BORING Monday, something unexpected happened that pulled Boubou and Aya right into the middle of the counterfeiters' story.

That Monday afternoon, as the school bell rang, Boubou and Aya walked home, their backpacks bouncing. When they stepped inside, they saw something strange. There, in their living room, was Grandma Diouf. She was sitting on the edge of her chair, staring at a pile of money in her lap like it was some weird treasure.

Boubou, always ready with a joke, couldn't help himself. "Whoa, Grandma! Did you win the lottery or something?" But his smile faded when he saw how worried Grandma Diouf looked. Her hands were shaking as she moved the money to the table.

Aya, quick to notice when something was wrong, asked, "What's going on, Grandma? Is everything okay?"

Without saying anything, Grandma Diouf got up slowly and walked to the window. She looked out at the street for a moment, then turned to face her grandkids with hope and worry on her face.

"Did either of you see anyone selling rugs in the neighborhood this afternoon?" she asked, sounding desperate.

Boubou and Aya looked at each other, confused, and shook their heads. "We just came straight from school, Grandma. Didn't see anyone weird," they said. But then Boubou's eyes widened as he realized something. "Wait a minute, the rug!" he exclaimed. "You sold our old rug, didn't you?"

The Diouf family living room had always had a super soft rug from a faraway place. This rug had its own story. Mr. Diouf had bought it on a whim during a trip to the city but later wished he hadn't.

Malik Diouf, trying to surprise his wife, had brought the rug home without realizing its color didn't match anything in their living room. He'd forgotten to think about what the room already looked like, which is something dads often do. The rug's color was nothing like what Mrs. Diouf wanted for their living room. And, because Mr. Diouf had bought it at a special no-returns sale, they were stuck with it.

Over the years, Mrs. Diouf often talked about getting a new rug that she liked better. She had always imagined something different for their living room floor, but they never got around to changing it. Sadly, both she and Mr. Diouf passed away before they could get a new rug.

Over the years, people had offered to buy the rug, but never for what it was really worth. The highest offer had been only $100, which Mrs. Diouf thought was ridiculous. "I'm not selling a $500 rug for such a tiny amount," she'd say, feeling proud and annoyed at the same time. So the rug stayed put, quietly out of place in the Diouf family's living room.

"How much did they pay you for it?" Aya asked.

Grandma Diouf's answer was simple but shocking. "I gave it away."

"Gave it away?" Both kids echoed, not believing their ears.

Grandma Diouf nodded solemnly. "Not on purpose, though. I got tricked."

Boubou's worry grew. "Tricked? How?" he asked urgently.

Grandma Diouf pointed at the pile of money. "I went to the bank to put this money in—"

"You don't mean it's fake, do you?" Aya cut in, her eyes wide.

"The bank teller said it was," Grandma Diouf replied, sounding defeated.

Boubou flopped into a chair, looking frustrated and confused. "I can't believe this! How did you get tricked? And for how much?" he asked, sounding both worried and angry.

Grandma Diouf's answer was serious. "$400."

Aya whistled softly, shocked. "But how did it all happen?" she asked, wanting to know every detail.

"He showed up right after you two left for school," Grandma Diouf began. "It must have been just before two o'clock."

"Who was he?" Aya asked, leaning in closer.

"This rug buyer, he was a strange little man — short and skinny. Definitely not from around here. You could tell by how he looked and talked. His English wasn't very good. He had these small, dark eyes that looked really intense. He came right up to the front door, asking if I wanted to buy any rugs. When I said no, he changed his tune and asked if I had any rugs to sell. Said he was a traveling rug merchant, going from city to city, buying and selling rugs."

"So, did you tell him about our living room rug?" Boubou asked, trying to figure out what happened next.

"I only thought of it then," Grandma Diouf continued. "It seemed like the perfect chance to finally get rid of that rug, just like your mother always wanted. Maybe even get something better to replace it. I told him about our rug, but I warned him that he might not be able to afford it."

"And he still wanted to see it?" Boubou guessed.

"When I doubted he could afford it, he just laughed, kind of sly-like," Grandma Diouf said. "He bragged that money was no problem for him. Said he'd bought rugs for as much as $1,000 and still made a profit. So, I invited him in to see our rug. As soon as he saw it, he couldn't stop praising it. He asked me how much I wanted, and I aimed high, saying $500. I didn't really expect that much, but you know, these traders always try to bargain you down, so you've got to start high."

Boubou and Aya grinned at each other, appreciating their grandmother's smart thinking.

"He wasn't willing to pay $500, but he offered $300," she went on. "I told him that was too low. Then I asked if he had any rugs he'd trade for it. He seemed unsure about that idea. He said he had some medium-priced rugs but nothing worth as much as ours."

"Did he say where he kept these other rugs?" Boubou asked, trying to understand how the stranger operated.

"He mentioned that his other rugs were at his hotel, but the really valuable ones were all back in the city. He said it would take a day or two to have them brought here," Grandma Diouf explained. "But he offered to buy our rug for $400, taking a chance that he could sell me a high-quality rug later when he got his shipment from the city."

"That sounds fair," Aya commented, nodding thoughtfully.

"It did seem reasonable at the time," Grandma Diouf agreed. "After all, the rug was probably worth around $400, maybe even less since we'd been using it for years. And I didn't have to buy another rug from him unless I wanted to, so I said yes. He paid me right then and there."

"$400!" Boubou exclaimed, amazed.

"Yes, in cash," Grandma Diouf continued. "He had a lot of money in a big, bulky leather wallet. He gave me the money in $10 and $50 bills. I felt pretty proud of myself for making such a good deal."

Boubou's voice got serious. "Until you went to put the money in the bank," he said.

"That's exactly what happened," Grandma Diouf said, sounding frustrated and shocked. "The bank teller barely looked at the bills before telling me he couldn't take them. I was confused at first, totally forgetting about all the rumors of fake money going around. But then he explained they were counterfeit. I had no choice but to come back home, realizing I'd been cleverly tricked."

Boubou, always trying to find the bright side, chimed in, "But maybe you weren't tricked, Grandma. Maybe the rug buyer didn't know the money was fake. Did he tell you which hotel he was staying at?"

"Yes, he gave me the name," Grandma Diouf replied. "But I've already called the police. They checked for me, and it turns out there's been no rug buyer staying at that hotel or any other in town, as far as they could tell."

Boubou's face fell as he took in this information. "That doesn't sound good at all."

"What's even worse," Grandma Diouf continued, "is that the police found out he had caught the early afternoon train out of town. And he wasn't just carrying our rug; he had another one with him, which he had tricked another woman in town into selling."

"He must be planning to sell them in another city," Aya guessed, trying to follow the con man's plan.

"That's exactly what he did," Grandma Diouf confirmed. "They found he'd bought a ticket to the next city. The police there said he'd already sold both rugs to a big rug store and then disappeared. He got $300 for our rug and $200 for the other."

Boubou was bursting with curiosity. "Did he pay the other woman with fake money too?"

"Yes, he did," Grandma Diouf replied, sounding disappointed.

Boubou shook his head, thinking about the rug buyer's scheme. "He made quite a bit of money that afternoon. And he sure didn't waste any time getting away, either."

"If only I had gone to the bank earlier," Grandma Diouf said regretfully. "I got there just before three, and by the time I called the police, they started looking into it here and then traced where he went in the next city... Well, you know how slow the police can be. By then, it was already too late."

Boubou thought about the situation. "I guess the chances of him coming back in two days with that rug he promised are pretty much zero," he said. "He's either working with the counterfeiters, or he got stuck with a bunch of fake money himself and decided to pass it on as cleverly as he could."

Grandma Diouf looked really down about the whole thing. "I should've been more careful," she admitted with a sigh. "I just wanted to do what your mother always wanted and replace this old rug. With all the fake money going around lately, I should've been extra cautious, especially with $400. It might be my own fault, but it really hurts to lose so much money." She looked at the pile of worthless bills on the table. "It's completely useless."

Boubou picked up one of the fake bills and looked at it closely. "This looks exactly like the fake $50 bill that guy at the station gave to Aya and me," he said, feeling the paper. "I bet it's from the same bunch."

Aya couldn't help but sound upset and frustrated. "$400! That's the biggest scam yet. If I could just get my hands on that rug merchant, I'd shake every last dollar out of him."

Boubou nodded in agreement but sounded more realistic. "It's not likely we'll catch him now. He's sold the rugs and made a clean getaway."

Grandma Diouf stayed quiet, clearly upset about losing the money. Not only was the rug valuable, but being tricked, especially after all the warnings about fake money, really stung. The rug merchant had seemed so believable, and Grandma Diouf, who usually trusted people, hadn't suspected a thing.

Boubou stood up, determined even though the chances were slim. "We'll go talk to the police," he suggested. "Though, I doubt it'll change much."

Aya laughed a little sarcastically and added, "Chief Gaye will probably say he's busy following leads. And that's probably as far as it'll go."

Their visit to the police station went exactly as Aya and Boubou thought it would. When they got there, they found Chief Gaye and Detective Diallo totally wrapped up in a card game, clearly more interested in their hands than in solving the case.

When the kids brought up the sneaky rug seller, Chief Gaye just shook his head. "We're looking into some leads," he said, trying to sound serious even though he was still staring at his cards. "But so far, we haven't found any more clues about where he went."

Detective Diallo nodded, putting on a big frown. "Not a single trace," he added dramatically.

Boubou, still hoping a little, asked, "Do you think you'll actually catch him?"

Chief Gaye answered more confidently this time. "Of course we'll catch him," he said. "Didn't I just say we're following some clues? We'll have him locked up, no doubt about it."

Detective Diallo, barely looking away from his cards, chimed in, "I'm personally working on this case." But he didn't sound very convincing.

"Leave it to us, kids," Chief Gaye said, hardly glancing up from the game. "Your move, Diallo."

Aya and Boubou looked at each other, rolling their eyes. It was clear the police weren't going to be much help.

As Aya and Boubou walked out of the police station, they both felt pretty sure that the local cops weren't exactly working overtime to catch the sneaky rug seller. They shared a look that said, "Can you believe this?"

"Well, that was a waste of time," Aya muttered, kicking a pebble on the sidewalk.

Boubou nodded, his face scrunched up in thought. "I don't think they're going to do much about this at all. Did you see how they barely looked up from their card game?"

"Yeah," Aya agreed. "It's like they care more about who wins at cards than catching bad guys!"

As they walked home, both kids were quiet for a while, thinking about what had happened. Finally, Boubou broke the silence.

"You know what, Aya? I think if we want to solve this mystery, we're going to have to do it ourselves."

Aya's eyes lit up. "You're right! We could be like those kid detectives in the books we read. We're probably smarter than those lazy cops anyway."

"Exactly!" Boubou grinned. "Let's make a plan. We can start by retracing Grandma's steps and looking for clues the police might have missed."

"And we should keep our eyes and ears open around town," Aya added. "Someone might have seen something useful."

As they reached their front door, both kids were buzzing with excitement about their new mission.

"Operation Catch the Rug Thief is officially underway," Boubou declared dramatically.

Aya laughed. "Let's just hope we can pull it off without getting into too much trouble."

With that, they headed inside, their minds already racing with ideas for how to crack the case and bring the cunning rug seller to justice. Little did they know, their amateur sleuthing was about to lead them into an adventure bigger than they could have imagined.

✳ ✳ ✳

CHAPTER TWENTY

The Anonymous Ultimatum

THREE DAYS LATER, SOMETHING STRANGE HAPPENED AT THE Diouf house. Malik Diouf, who had passed away a while ago, got a mysterious note. It was weird because, well, he wasn't exactly around to read it anymore.

That day, no one saw who left the note. The Diouf kids were at the pier, super excited about their boat race with Pierre and Adama. They'd been talking about it non-stop for days. Meanwhile, Grandma Diouf was in the kitchen, cooking up a storm. The whole house smelled amazing, like a warm hug made of food.

Suddenly, the doorbell rang. It was so loud it even cut through the clatter of pots and pans in the kitchen. Grandma Diouf wiped her floury hands on her apron and went to answer it.

When she opened the door, no one was there. She looked out at the street. On the other side, a man was walking away quickly. A young woman was strolling by, gently rocking a baby. Further down, two guys were having what looked like a pretty intense chat on the corner.

Grandma Diouf was confused. Had she imagined the doorbell? She was about to go back inside when something caught her eye. A white thing had landed at her feet.

Curious, she bent down to pick it up. It was an envelope, plain and a bit worn out, sealed shut. The name Malik Diouf was written on it. The simple envelope with that name on it made the whole thing feel mysterious and important.

She looked at it for a moment, her fingers tracing over the name, then took it inside. She put it carefully on the desk in her late son's study, a room that still felt like he might walk in at any moment.

Letters like this weren't totally weird for the Diouf house. When her son was alive and working as a detective, they'd get anonymous tips and strange messages all the time. These notes would show up like little mystery birds, some with useful info, others just nonsense. He was great at figuring out which was which. Mr. and Mrs. Diouf, who had passed away a few years ago, still got mail sometimes too, since not everyone knew they were gone.

Grandma Diouf figured this envelope was probably another piece of some detective puzzle. That might explain why whoever left it ran away so fast after ringing the bell.

Aya and Boubou didn't get home until late afternoon. Their day had been one big adventure.

As they got close to the pier, Aya suddenly changed direction, heading towards the fish market. She felt a weird pull, like someone was whispering directions only she could hear. Feeling like something big was about to happen, she turned to Boubou, her eyes sparkling with excitement.

"Come on," she said, "follow me!"

Boubou hesitated, looking confused. He was curious about why Aya suddenly changed plans. Still, he was also thinking about what they were supposed to be doing.

"But Aya, what about our boat race with Pierre and Adama? We can't be late," he reminded her.

Aya wasn't backing down. "Trust me on this one, Boubou. There's something important here. We need to check it out," she insisted, feeling drawn to the fish market like a magnet.

Boubou might have been puzzled, but he knew better than to doubt Aya's hunches. These weird whispers she seemed to hear had helped them solve mysteries before. He nodded, showing he trusted her, and followed his sister. They picked up the pace as they entered the busy market, the boat race temporarily forgotten as a new mystery unfolded.

When they got to the harbor, their detective senses went into overdrive. Aya was right - something was up. They followed a suspicious-looking man to the fish market and watched him secretly hand a small package to a woman dressed all in black. The woman then disappeared into the crowd. The kids recognized her but decided to play it cool. They didn't want to scare her off and blow their cover. It was a smart move - they could always talk to her later.

After their brush with the mysterious woman, Aya and Boubou headed to the pier. They parked their bikes by the dock and hopped onto their boat, the Mystery. As they sailed into the bay for their thrilling race with Pierre and Adama, it felt like a quick break from all the detective work - a chance to just be kids having fun, even with all the secrets and mysteries swirling around them.

Just then, Boubou and Aya burst into the house, their faces red from laughing and having fun out on the bay. They were cracking up as they told the story of what happened to Adama Sambou.

"You should've seen it!" Boubou exclaimed. "Adama tried to do this crazy stunt on the front of the motorboat—"

"And he ended up falling right into the water!" Aya finished, giggling.

"Yeah, he was soaked!" Boubou added. "But get this - he just hopped on his motorcycle with that funny little sidecar, dripping wet, and drove off!"

Aya tried to copy Adama's cheerful voice. "He was like, 'Well, I skipped my bath last night, so I guess this makes up for it!' Can you believe it? Eww!"

Grandma Diouf listened to their story, laughing along with them. She could just picture poor Adama, all wet but still in good spirits. After a moment, she remembered something, and her face got a bit more serious.

"You know, something weird happened today," she said, trying to sound casual but clearly interested. "Someone left a letter here for your dad. The doorbell rang, but when I went to check, no one was there. Just this letter on the ground." She pointed towards the study. "I put it on the desk in there. It's strange, right? You'd think after all this time, people would know he's... not here anymore. Oh well..."

Aya and Boubou looked at each other, their eyes lighting up with excitement. Without saying a word, they raced into the study.

The letter sat on the desk, looking innocent but full of mystery. Boubou, trying to act cool, carefully opened the envelope and pulled out a single, flimsy piece of paper. The message was scribbled in pencil like someone had written it in a hurry.

As Boubou read the note, a slow smile spread across his face. He passed the paper to Aya. "Looks like someone's trying to scare us," he said, sounding almost amused.

Aya read the messy handwriting:

"You should really think about dropping this fake case, or you might lose more than you expect. We know all about these tricks. Take this as a friendly warning. And Panko? He's not involved. It would be smart to leave him out of it."

She looked worried when she finished reading. Looking up at Boubou, she asked, "What should we do about this?"

Boubou shrugged like it was no big deal. "We'll ignore it, of course," he said.

"But what if they try to hurt us?" Aya sounded a little scared.

"They might try," Boubou admitted, still sounding calm. "But they wouldn't be the first to try scaring us off a case. Remember all those threats Dad used to get?"

"Yeah, he'd just laugh and throw them away."

"And that's exactly what we're going to do," Boubou said firmly. He was trying to remind Aya that facing scary stuff was part of what their family did, just like their dad used to.

"But they must be close by to deliver a note like this," Aya pointed out.

"Remember, we always thought their hideout was around here, right? Don't worry, Aya. I'm not scared of them. Are you?"

"It's Grandma I'm worried about. These guys are mean. They'd do anything."

Boubou chuckled. "We've dealt with threats before. This is just another trick to scare us. We're sticking with the case—even though we haven't figured out much yet."

"Still, this note is like adding insult to injury. First, the crooks trick Grandma out of $400 with their fake money, and now they're trying to scare us off the case."

Boubou looked at the note one more time before carefully putting it back in the envelope.

✳ ✳ ✳

CHAPTER TWENTY ONE

Shadows In The Moonlight

Boubou and Aya pedaled quickly through the countryside. As the clock ticked closer to ten, they neared the abandoned path leading to the Cazamoun River. Riding side by side, they planned their next steps.

"Let's leave our bikes where we did last time when we went to the old power plant," Boubou suggested.

Aya frowned, thinking hard. "I wish we could hide them closer to the river. If we need to make a quick escape, they'd be handy. But we can't risk anyone hearing us coming."

Her brother nodded, his eyes scanning the quiet night. "You're right. It's so quiet out here you could probably hear a bicycle from a mile away on this bumpy road. Even though they're new, they'd rattle like crazy on these old stones."

"Yeah," Aya chimed in with a grin. "We'd sound like a bunch of pots and pans having a dance party!"

Boubou chuckled softly. "Exactly. Stealth mode it is, then. We'll have to rely on our ninja-like sneaking skills from here on out."

As they continued pedaling, the siblings fell into a comfortable silence, each lost in thoughts of the scary adventure ahead.

Hiding their bikes under some nearby trees, Boubou and Aya continued on foot. The moon hung high in the sky, turning the road ahead into a glowing silver ribbon.

"I kinda wish it was darker," Aya whispered, her eyes darting around. "We'll have to be extra sneaky as we get closer."

"Yeah," Boubou agreed. "There might be guards around. But we'll get a better idea once we're there."

As they reached the top of a hill, they saw the Cazamoun River spread out before them. Moonlight sparkled on the water, making it look magical. Willow trees lined the banks, their droopy branches creating deep shadows. A light mist floated over the fields, making everything look dreamy and mysterious.

The old power plant stood out against the night sky like a spooky castle. It was right next to the river, near where the old canal glimmered in the moonlight. The building was completely dark and looked totally abandoned.

"Maybe everyone's gone," Aya said hopefully.

Boubou shook his head. "Remember, it was all boarded up last time. I bet they're still in there."

Moving carefully, the siblings started down the hill, wrapped in the night's secrets.

❖

Boubou and Aya crept through the trees, avoiding the open field between the woods and the old power plant. The night was so quiet that even whispers felt too loud. They could hear the distant rumble of rapids and a waterfall, making everything feel spooky and exciting.

At the edge of the trees, about 200 feet from the building, they stopped to look around.

"We need to cross that open space," Boubou whispered, barely audible.

"Then what?" Aya asked softly.

"See that willow tree by the plant?" Boubou pointed. "It goes right up to the roof. If we can climb it, we might be able to drop onto the roof or sneak through a window."

Aya nodded, her eyes following the path. "As long as we can climb without making noise."

"That's the tricky part," Boubou replied. "But getting across this open space is the biggest challenge."

The moonlit grass stretched out before them like a silvery stage. Crossing it meant risking being seen by anyone watching from the power plant. But they had no choice; the plant stood alone by the river with no cover on this side.

"We have to crawl across," Boubou whispered. "Ready?"

Aya nodded, looking determined. "Ready."

"Move slow and quiet. If you hear anything weird, freeze."

On hands and knees, they left the safety of the trees. They began inching carefully towards the willow tree behind the plant.

Every move was risky. The moon made everything super bright, and it felt like every single blade of grass was lit up.

Halfway across, they heard a loud clang of a door. Boubou whispered, "Freeze!" and they flattened themselves in the grass.

A gruff voice came from the power plant. "I saw someone on the hillside."

The siblings' hearts raced, but they stayed perfectly still, knowing they had to be quiet and not move.

Another voice answered, sounding doubtful. "You're seeing things, Mako. There's nobody out there."

But Mako insisted, "I tell you, I saw someone crawling through the grass. I'm sure of it. I saw him from that upper window."

"Where?" asked the second voice.

"Out there—look! Can't you see something dark up there?" Mako sounded worried.

There was a pause, then a laugh from the second man. "It's just a log."

"It's not a log," Mako argued. "Logs don't move."

"That thing isn't moving."

"It was moving earlier."

"If you're so sure, why don't you go check?" the second man teased. "You've been jumpy lately, always thinking you see people sneaking around."

"I have good reasons to be careful. This place isn't safe anymore. We should've left a week ago."

"This is as safe as it gets," the other man said.

"Safe? Ever since those two kids started asking Kirabo questions, I've been worried. They're onto us. They were even at the train station when I gave the package to Jango. I bet they saw me."

"They're just kids," the second man scoffed. "You worry too much."

"I'm going to check that 'log' on the hill," Mako decided.

Hidden in the grass, Boubou and Aya looked at each other, super nervous. They heard Mako's footsteps moving away from the plant. They knew they had to stay as still as possible to avoid being caught.

Luckily, there was a real log near Boubou. But he knew if Mako came too close, they'd be in big trouble. They couldn't run yet, not until they absolutely had to. Boubou felt sad, thinking their mission might end before they even reached the power plant.

Then, as if by magic, help came from nature itself. A dark cloud started to cover the moon, turning the bright hillside into a world of shadows.

Boubou whispered urgently to Aya, "Now's our chance! To the willow tree!"

They jumped up and ran towards the willow tree behind the old power plant. Their feet were super quiet on the grass. It was risky—Mako might still see them—but they had to take the chance while it was dark.

Mako had just stepped out of the power plant and couldn't see well in the sudden darkness. This gave Boubou and Aya just enough time. They reached the safety of the willow tree just as the moon came out again, making everything bright once more.

Out of breath, they paused under the tree, watching Mako. They saw him walk to where they had been, kick at something in the grass – probably the log – and then turn back, muttering to himself.

From the doorway, the other man called out, "Well, what was it?"

"It was a log," Mako admitted. "But I swear it moved earlier."

"Maybe you need glasses," the man at the door joked.

Mako didn't laugh. He walked back to the power plant, and Boubou and Aya heard his last words.

"You might think I'm being too careful," Mako said, sounding frustrated and worried. "But we have good reasons to be. Think about what'll happen if we get caught."

"Twenty years in jail, sure, but we're not getting caught," the other man said confidently.

"Don't be so sure," Mako argued. "We can't take any chances. I'd rather be wrong about a few logs than end up in jail because I felt too safe."

"I guess you have a point. But tonight, at least, everything seems okay."

"I'm still going to check around the building," Mako said.

"You really are nervous," the other man remarked.

"Yes, I am," Mako snapped. "I always get jumpy when I think I see something sneaking in from the woods. Log or not, I saw movement."

"It was probably just an animal, like a sheep, cow, or dog," the other man suggested.

"Maybe it was a dog," Mako agreed, but he still sounded unsure.

"We should get back to work. Dogo's waiting for us."

"I'll walk around the plant, just to be sure," Mako said.

"Go ahead. I'll be inside with Dogo," his friend replied.

Boubou and Aya, hiding by the willow tree, listened carefully to Mako's heavy footsteps as he left the doorway. Soon, they saw his dark shape in the moonlight as he walked around the building.

The siblings pressed themselves closer to the tree, ducking their heads to hide their faces. They were wearing dark clothes and caps, and they stayed super still, knowing that any movement or a glimpse of their pale faces might give them away.

They got more and more nervous as they heard Mako coming closer. He seemed to be looking carefully, poking through the junk at the side of the building. It was clear he wasn't convinced that what he saw moving on the hill was just his imagination. He was making absolutely sure no one was hiding near the old power plant.

For Boubou and Aya, each second felt like forever. They were caught in a tense, silent waiting game, hoping Mako would finish his check and go away so they could continue their risky mission.

Mako got closer and closer. The branches of the willow tree rustled as he brushed against them. He was now just a few yards away, dangerously close.

Boubou and Aya stood completely still, not daring to move or even look up. The tension was so thick you could cut it with a knife.

Then, Mako's footsteps stopped. He was standing nearby, scarily close, in complete silence. It seemed like he was listening, maybe sensing something was off.

The big question hung in the air: Had Mako spotted them?

✳ ✳ ✳

CHAPTER TWENTY TWO

In The Heart Of Darkness

Aya and Boubou held their breath under the willow tree, feeling like time had stopped. They were so close to Mako that they could almost touch him, hidden only by the tree's drooping branches. Every second felt like a year as they wondered: Had he seen them?

Their hearts pounded like drums as they waited. Then, Mako let out a grunt that sounded like he was happy with something. They listened, barely daring to breathe, as his footsteps slowly faded away in the opposite direction. They weren't in the clear yet, but hope was on the horizon.

It felt like forever before Aya and Boubou even thought about moving. Finally, gathering all their courage, they peeked around the tree trunk. Mako was nowhere in sight. They listened closely as he walked around the old power plant building, his steps echoing in the quiet air.

At last, they heard what they were waiting for – the power plant door slammed shut. Mako was back inside. Aya and Boubou let out a huge sigh of relief. They were safe… for now.

"Whew! That was way too close," Aya whispered, her voice shaky but relieved.

"Shh!" Boubou hissed, his eyes darting around. "Not so loud. They might still have their ears open."

The duo stayed still a bit longer, making extra sure the coast was clear before planning their next move. The willow tree had been their superhero hideout, but now it was time to figure out what to do next.

Aya and Boubou huddled in the shadows, waiting. Time seemed to crawl as the moon kept watch overhead. Finally, it looked like Mako had given up searching. Just as they started to relax, a weird sound came from inside the old power plant. It was a strange whirring noise, followed by the muffled rumbling of machines.

"What's that?" Aya whispered, her voice tiny.

They listened hard. The rumbling sound went up and down like a strange robot ocean. Boubou, always spotting things, gently poked his sister and pointed at the power plant. Halfway up the wall was a window covered with boards. Through a tiny crack, a sliver of light peeked out.

"Look there," Boubou breathed. "That's gotta be the power room."

The mysterious machine noises kept going. Aya felt a surge of excitement and whispered, "We're super lucky! They must do their secret stuff at night."

Boubou nodded, his eyes glued to the faint light. "But we need to be totally sure," he added, his brain already cooking up plans.

"How do we sneak in there?" Aya wondered, staring at the big building.

Boubou, always the thinker, had an idea. "The willow tree. We climb up, then jump onto the roof."

Aya frowned. "What if they hear us? We'd be toast!"

But Boubou was sure of his plan. "They won't hear a thing. Those walls are super thick brick. Plus, all that machine noise? It's like our own personal invisibility cloak for sound. It's our best shot to get inside."

"Okay, you go first, I'll follow."

With that, Boubou crept towards the willow tree, its branches dancing slightly in the night breeze.

❖

Climbing the tree was tough. It was huge, but the branches bent dangerously under Boubou's weight. They realized it was too risky for both of them to climb at once, so Aya stayed on the ground, keeping watch while Boubou tackled the tricky climb.

Up and up he went, the branches getting wobblier the higher he climbed. Finally, Boubou reached the top branches that hung over the power plant's roof. With a careful swing, he positioned himself above the building, his feet searching for a good spot on the slanted roof. After a scary moment, he found his balance. He let go of the branch, which sprang back with a soft swoosh.

Boubou froze, listening hard. No alarms, no shouts – nobody had noticed him. His heart raced with excitement as he signaled to Aya. It was her turn now.

Boubou's soft call was answered by the quiet rustling of branches as Aya started climbing. In the faint moonlight, he could just see her shadow moving through the springy willow branches. Like a pro climber, Aya swung from the tree and landed gracefully next to her brother on the old power plant's roof.

"We need to find a way in," Boubou whispered, looking around. "There's gotta be a trapdoor up here somewhere. If not, we'll have to try one of the upper windows. I saw a small one open at the front. But let's hope for a trapdoor."

Moving across the roof was easier than they thought. Even though it was steep, they could walk okay on the old shingles. But the roof was in bad shape. At one point, Boubou almost fell into a big hole where the shingles had rotted away, reminding them how old and unused the power plant was.

They searched everywhere but couldn't find a trapdoor. Aya and Boubou looked at each other, disappointed but determined. It looked like they'd have to use one of the upper windows instead.

Suddenly, Boubou's eyes lit up, and he pointed to the hole in the roof. "We'll go through here," he said.

The hole was small, only about a foot wide, but when Boubou shone his flashlight down, they could see an attic-like space below – the top part of the abandoned power plant. Without a word, they started carefully pulling at the weak roof. The weather had already done most of the work, making the roof easy to break. Shingle by shingle, they carefully made the opening bigger, turning the small gap into a hole big enough for a person.

Instead of just throwing the broken pieces away, they carefully stacked them on the roof. They moved slowly and quietly, trying not to make any noise. It took a while, but finally, they had a gap wide enough to fit through.

Boubou went first, carefully lowering himself through the hole they'd made. The attic was super cramped, with a ceiling only five feet high. When his feet touched the wooden floor, he tested it to make sure it wouldn't break. Satisfied, he crouched down and used his flashlight to look around, searching for a way to get to the lower floors of the plant.

The building was in pretty bad shape, and it was too risky for both of them to be inside on this rickety floor.

Being extra careful, Boubou whispered up to Aya, "Stay on the roof for now. It's not safe in here yet."

"But why?" Aya whispered back, her voice tinged with concern.

"The floor's really old and creaky," Boubou explained softly. "If we're both in here, it might break. I'll check it out first and let you know when it's okay to come down."

Aya nodded, understanding the danger. "Okay, but be careful," she whispered.

At first, Boubou's search seemed useless. The room looked like a closed box, cut off from the rest of the power plant. Solid floorboards were everywhere, with no sign of stairs or a way out. Boubou felt crushed. They were so close, but now they were stuck in a tiny attic.

But then, he spotted something – a faint line, a crack between the boards. He shone his flashlight on it and saw a square outline about two feet wide. A trapdoor! Excited, he carefully pried at the edges, slowly working one side loose. Finally, he lifted and removed the trapdoor, putting it aside super quietly.

This discovery gave him new hope. There was a way deeper into the power plant, and they were one step closer to uncovering its secrets. The darkness below the trapdoor was thick, like a heavy blanket. Boubou quickly shone his flashlight down, revealing a ladder going to another room below. That quick look was enough to know what to do next.

He whispered up to Aya, "All clear. Come on down."

Through the roof's opening, he watched Aya's shadow appear. She skillfully climbed down into the attic next to him. Having her there made him feel braver.

"I found a way down," Boubou whispered. "There's a trapdoor here."

Aya's eyes sparkled with curiosity, even in the dim light. "Where does it go?"

Boubou pointed to the trapdoor. "There's another room right below us, and it's empty. I bet the power room is right under that. And look," he said, pointing to a door in the far wall of the lower room, "that probably leads to stairs going down to the main part of the plant."

Aya nodded, getting the plan. "So, are we going?"

Boubou looked at her, his eyes determined. "Yeah, let's find out what's really happening in this old power plant. We've been lucky so far. Nobody knows we're here."

He gave the flashlight to Aya so she could see better while he tackled the trapdoor. Carefully feeling his way, he found the top of the ladder with his foot. The ladder made a creaky noise under his weight, which sounded super loud in the quiet, but it held strong.

Boubou went down slowly, being extra quiet. His brain was working hard, figuring out the layout of the power plant. From the bit of light he'd seen earlier through the window, he guessed that the counterfeiters' power room was probably in the middle of the building, right under the room he was entering. The building got bigger as it reached the ground floor, so Boubou thought the counterfeiters were using both this room and the one right above it.

Finally, his feet touched the floor below without a sound.

Boubou looked up through the trapdoor and whispered, "Coast is clear Aya. You can come down now."

"Are you sure it's safe?" Aya whispered back.

"Yeah, I'm standing on solid ground," Boubou assured her. "Just take it slow and quiet, okay?"

"Got it," Aya replied softly. "I'm on my way."

A few moments later, he heard the tiniest noise above as Aya started climbing down.

The rumble of machines vibrated through the floor, telling them they were right above where all the action was happening. Muffled voices mixed with machine sounds proved that Boubou was right: the power room, which was probably the center of the counterfeiters' operation, was just below them.

Aya reached the bottom of the ladder without making a sound, showing how sneaky they both were. The dark room wrapped around them, hiding all the secrets they were about to uncover.

Boubou took the flashlight and turned it on to see where they were. They stood in an empty room with a low ceiling. Across the room, a doorway led to a staircase that went down to a landing and then kept going down into the plant. The room below probably opened onto this landing.

As Boubou memorized these details, which could be super important for a quick escape if needed, Aya's whisper caught his attention. He spun around to see her crouched down, staring at a crack in the floorboards. She waved for him to come over quickly.

Moving quietly, Boubou knelt beside Aya and peeked through the crack. The tiny view showed them a glimpse of the world below – a sneak peek at what they were about to face.

CHAPTER TWENTY THREE

In The Belly Of The Beast

BOUBOU CROUCHED NEXT TO HIS SISTER, MOVING AS quietly as a cat on the prowl. With a quick twist, he switched off the flashlight, and darkness swallowed them whole. But a thin streak of light peeked through a crack in the floor, hinting at secrets hidden below.

Heart pounding like a drum, Boubou pressed his eye to the gap. What he saw made his jaw drop to the floor. Uncle Dogo, his old buddy, and Mako were huddled around a small printing press in the dusty basement of the abandoned power plant. Their sleeves were rolled up, and their aprons were splattered with ink like abstract paintings gone wild.

The press hummed steadily, like a mechanical lullaby, as Mako carefully fed it sheets of weird reddish paper. But it was the table next to the press that really caught Boubou and Aya's attention.

Mountains of crisp, new bills covered the table, neatly wrapped in paper bands like presents waiting to be opened. The numbers on them ranged from $5 to $500. It was like stumbling into a treasure cave straight out of an adventure movie, except this treasure was definitely not the real deal.

"They're making fake money," Boubou whispered, barely able to keep his voice down. He felt like his insides were doing cartwheels.

Aya nodded, her eyes as wide as dinner plates. Even though they knew the money was fake, seeing all those freshly printed red bills was kind of amazing. It was like looking at a fortune, even if it wasn't real.

They could only see a small part of the room through their peephole, but by shifting around a bit, they pieced together what was happening. Over the whirr of the printing press, they could hear the three men talking, their voices drifting up like smoke.

"We'll be living large once we get rid of this batch," Uncle Dogo said, sounding pretty pleased with himself.

"If we can get rid of it all," Mako grumbled, always the party pooper.

"Oh, we will," the third guy chimed in, confident as a rooster. "It's been smooth sailing so far. Jango and his crew have been doing a good job, right?"

"Yeah, but they should stay away from Zinguichou," Mako warned, his voice tense. "People might start wondering where all this money's coming from."

"Why would they?" Uncle Dogo asked, cool as a cucumber. "We're not just hitting Zinguichou, you know."

"That Toto Panko almost blew our cover, though," someone pointed out, sounding annoyed.

"But he doesn't know what we're really up to," Uncle Dogo said, brushing off the concern. "He might think we're hanging around the old plant, but he's not sure. He won't snitch."

"Still," Mako said, sounding as worried as a long-tailed cat in a room full of rocking chairs, "I'll feel better when we're done here and far away. This story about special batteries might fool some people, but the locals are getting nosy. The farmers are gossiping because we're not dealing with them."

"Let them gossip. We're leaving soon anyway," Uncle Dogo said, waving away the concern. "That new photo you made for us is awesome. It looks so real, only an expert could tell the difference. We'll make $50,000 easy with those tens."

Mako finally sounded happy, like a kid with a new toy. "It did turn out pretty good. But I've always said our paper feels off—too light. It needs to be a bit thicker to feel like real money. Real bills have more weight to them."

"What's eating you tonight, Mako?" Uncle Dogo asked, sounding annoyed. "You've been jumpy all evening. First, you're seeing things around the plant, and now you're worried about getting caught. By this time next week, we'll be rich, thanks to the biggest fake money scheme Africa's ever seen. You should be proud. When this is all over, we'll each have $15,000."

"That's why we need to be careful," Mako shot back, quick as a whip. "In a job like this, one mistake can ruin everything."

"But have we ever messed up? Who'd guess we're working out of this old power plant? The Diouf kids, the local detective's kids, are right in Zinguichou and haven't figured it out. Even the government guys are looking in the wrong place, thinking we're set up in the woods near Zabrousse."

"Using this old plant was pretty smart," Mako admitted, giving credit where it was due. "But the sooner we leave, the better."

"We'll finish printing tonight. We'll take off first thing tomorrow and come back for the machinery as soon as we can."

Boubou and Aya looked at each other, their eyes wide with realization. The counterfeiters were planning to leave earlier than they thought. It was like a ticking time bomb had just been set.

They kept watching through the cracks, feeling like spies in a movie, as the three men moved around. The printing press kept humming away, a steady beat to their secret operation. With each print, more fake bills joined the pile on the table, growing like a money mountain.

"Better than working for a living, right?" Uncle Dogo joked, looking at all the money they'd made with a grin as wide as a canyon.

"I'm going to travel the world with my share," the second man said, already dreaming of fancy vacations and exotic places.

"What about you, Mako?" Uncle Dogo asked, turning to his partner in crime.

"I'm hitting the race tracks," Mako boasted, puffing up like a proud rooster. "I'll tour every big one in Africa this year and double my money."

"You'll end up broke," the second man warned, shaking his head.

"No way," Mako said, confident as ever.

Uncle Dogo just smiled like he knew a secret. "We'll see. A lot of people have thought that and lost everything betting on horses."

Boubou and Aya finally understood what was going on, like puzzle pieces clicking into place. They'd seen the fake money operation with their own eyes, and now they knew why there had been so much counterfeit cash floating around lately. It was like uncovering a huge secret right under their noses.

Knowing the counterfeiters were about to finish up and disappear made Boubou and Aya realize they needed to act fast. It was now or never.

"Where are we going after this?" Mako asked, his voice drifting up to their hiding spot.

"We'll split up for a while," Uncle Dogo said, sounding like he had it all planned out. "Let's meet up in Zakar."

"Zakar? Where exactly?"

"We'll meet at Jango's place. You remember where he lives, right?" Uncle Dogo then mentioned an address in some neighborhood in the center. Boubou made sure to remember it, locking it away in his brain like a secret code. It might come in handy later if things didn't go as planned.

This new information made them realize they had to hurry. If they wanted to stop the operation, they had to do it now. It was like being in a race against time.

Standing up from their hiding spot, legs a bit wobbly from crouching so long, Boubou and Aya got ready to leave. Boubou pointed towards the exit that led to the landing, feeling like a general planning a battle.

"We need to go," he whispered urgently, his voice barely louder than a breath.

"What's the plan?" Aya whispered back, her eyes sparkling with excitement and fear.

"We need to get to Zinguichou for help," Boubou said, thinking fast. "We can't take them on by ourselves. It'd be like trying to catch a lion with a butterfly net."

"But how do we get out?" Aya pointed out, always the practical one. "The roof's too dangerous—we barely made it to the tree last time. I don't fancy becoming a pancake today."

"We'll use the stairs," Boubou suggested, trying to find the safest way out of this pickle.

"And just walk out the front door?" Aya asked, raising an eyebrow.

"Yeah, as quietly as we can," Boubou said, leading the way like a spy on a secret mission. "Like shadows in the night. They'll never know we were here."

Boubou and Aya moved like ninjas, each step as quiet as a mouse. Their sneakers were perfect for sneaking, barely making a sound on the floor. As they crept down the stairs, the printing press got louder, and they could hear the men talking more clearly.

Finally, they reached the important landing. A yellow light peeked out from under the workroom door like a warning sign, telling them danger was close. The stairs kept going down, leading deeper into the old power plant. It was their way out, but it was also super risky.

Holding their breath, they tiptoed past the workroom door. This was the scariest part - one little noise could give them away. But the printing press was so loud, and the bad guys were talking so much that they didn't hear Boubou and Aya sneaking by.

Boubou made it to the next set of stairs first, with Aya right behind him. Their hearts were pounding like drums, not just because they were scared of getting caught but because they were excited about uncovering such a big crime. It was like being in a real-life mystery movie!

In the dark power plant, Boubou and Aya carefully made their way towards the exit. Old machines loomed around them like sleeping giants, and the outline of the exit door was like a beacon of hope in the darkness.

But then, Boubou accidentally kicked a bucket someone had left on the stairs. The bucket went tumbling down, making a noise as loud as a herd of elephants! The sound echoed through the empty power plant like a giant alarm bell.

Realizing they were in big trouble, Boubou sprang into action. The noise was like a giant arrow pointing right at them, and they knew the bad guys would come looking.

With no time to try the exit door and hearing footsteps coming from upstairs, the siblings knew they had to hide and fast. Aya followed right behind Boubou as he ducked into a nearby room.

They found themselves in a room full of giant generators. In the dim light, the machines looked like huge, silent robots. The room had lots of places to hide, which was exactly what they needed right now.

From upstairs, they heard voices. A door opened, and a beam of light cut through the darkness. Mako's voice drifted down, sounding excited like a kid on a treasure hunt. "I'm sure I heard something!"

In the generator room, hiding in the shadows of the big machines, Boubou and Aya looked at each other. They didn't need to speak - they both knew they had to become invisible, like chameleons blending into the background.

"I'm going to find out what made that noise," Mako announced.

Boubou and Aya held their breath, hoping their hiding spot was good enough. It was like the most intense game of hide-and-seek ever, except this time, they really, really didn't want to be found!

✳ ✳ ✳

CHAPTER TWENTY FOUR

Black Cat's Luck

Boubou and Aya were trapped like mice in a corner. They could hear Mako's heavy boots thumping down the wooden stairs, each step making their hearts beat faster.

Boubou's eyes darted around the room. There was one window, but it was all boarded up. The only way out was the same door they'd come in through.

By now, Mako had reached the bottom of the stairs. The siblings heard him let out a surprised grunt as he found a bucket lying on its side.

"Found the culprit," he called up to someone upstairs. "Bucket took a tumble down the steps."

"So what?" Uncle Dogo's annoyed voice floated down.

"Someone must've knocked it over," Mako insisted.

"Don't be silly. There's no one else here. You're just being jumpy," Uncle Dogo shot back.

"Buckets don't walk themselves down stairs," Mako grumbled.

"Why don't you ask Kirabo? Maybe he did it," Uncle Dogo suggested, trying to pass the blame.

Everything went quiet as Mako walked into another room. To Boubou and Aya, the silence felt like it lasted forever. Finally, Mako came back.

"He's either out cold or faking it. I didn't wake him up. But something's fishy. I'm gonna look around anyway," he declared.

Mako's footsteps got closer to the generator room where Boubou and Aya were hiding. Quick as a flash, Boubou slipped behind the open door, pressing his back against the wall. Aya squeezed in next to him, barely breathing.

Mako stepped into the old generator room, shining his flashlight around. The beam swept across the walls, poking into every dusty corner. The siblings held their breath, praying he wouldn't think to look behind the door.

Suddenly, Mako muttered something under his breath. There was a rustling sound, and a shadow darted out from a corner.

"Meeow!"

"Just the stupid cat!" Mako grumbled.

The cat tried to be friendly, purring at Mako's feet, but he aimed a kick at it. Luckily, he missed. Grumpy and disappointed, he left the room empty-handed.

"Find anything?" Uncle Dogo called from the stairs, sounding impatient.

"Just the cat," Mako replied, frustrated. "Guess it was wandering around and caused all the fuss."

"Then get back up here and focus on what we're doing. See? I told you it was nothing," Uncle Dogo dismissed him.

Mako didn't answer, but they heard him going back upstairs. Soon, a door slammed, and the loud clunking and clattering of the printing press started up again.

Boubou let out a big breath he didn't know he'd been holding. "That was way too close," he whispered, his voice shaky with relief.

"Let's get out of here, now," he urged. "And that cat deserves a medal. How about a whole carton of milk for breakfast?"

Quiet as mice, they tiptoed out of the room and crept through the dark hallways of the old power plant. They headed straight for the front door. Just like Boubou had thought, it was locked from the inside. He reached out, found the bolt with his fingers, and slowly slid it open. The door creaked a little as they peeked outside into the dark night.

Boubou turned and put his finger to his lips, giving Aya the universal "Shh!" sign. Aya nodded, her eyes wide with excitement and a little bit of fear.

Suddenly, breaking the tense silence of their great escape, they heard a familiar sound from far away—a cat's meow. It was so unexpected and so perfectly timed that both of them couldn't help but grin. Aya had to clamp her hand over her mouth to keep from laughing out loud. The whole thing was just too funny!

They stepped outside, carefully closing the door behind them so no one would know they'd been there.

"Okay, now we've got to get to Zinguichou," Boubou whispered. "And we need to move fast!"

They weren't out of danger yet, but they'd managed to escape without getting caught, thanks to their furry little hero. The way ahead was clear, and with determination in their hearts, they set off into the night, racing to get back to their bikes.

They raced through the cool night, their feet barely touching the ground as they ran for the safety of the dark woods. Only when they were hidden under the trees did they dare to look back. The old power plant stood in the distance, looking scary and mysterious next to the shiny river. The bright moonlight made everything look almost ghostly.

"We'll be back," Aya said, her voice full of determination. She took one last look at the creepy outline of the power plant.

"And they're in for a big surprise before this night is over," Boubou added confidently, already thinking about their next move.

"I can't wait. Let's get going," Aya replied, still excited even after their close call earlier.

With new energy, they kept moving through the trees until they came out onto the empty road where they'd hidden their bikes. Quick as a flash, they jumped on and started pedaling fast.

They pedaled like the wind, racing through the night. Finally, the twinkling lights of the city appeared ahead. Their bikes zoomed along the shore road, bumped over dirt paths, and weaved through quiet city streets. Only a few trolleys and the odd taxi looking for late-night passengers were out.

At last, they reached home. They dropped their bikes and ran to the front door. Inside, Grandma Diouf was waiting up, looking worried.

"Where have you been? I was—" Grandma started to scold them.

But Boubou, out of breath and bursting with news, cut her off. "We found the counterfeiters!"

"The what?" Grandma's eyes went wide.

"The counterfeiters, Grandma. You need to call the police right now. We can catch them all tonight," Boubou insisted, his eyes shining with excitement.

"Is this true?" Grandma asked.

"Yes! We found where they're making fake money. If we hurry, the police can catch them red-handed. They don't know we were there," Boubou explained in a rush.

"And they're planning to leave first thing in the morning," Aya added quickly.

"Where is this happening?" Grandma demanded, already standing up.

"At the old power plant by the Cazamoun River. We just came from there!" Boubou said, his words tumbling out in excitement.

Grandma's eyes widened. "You were at the old power plant? At night? Do you have any idea how dangerous that was?"

Aya piped up, "We were careful, Grandma! We had to find out what was going on!"

"Yeah, and we didn't get caught," Boubou added quickly.

Grandma shook her head, a mix of worry and exasperation on her face. "You two are going to turn my hair white before its time. What if something had happened to you?"

"But Grandma, we found the counterfeiters!" Aya insisted.

Grandma sighed deeply. "I understand you were trying to help, but promise me you won't do anything like this again without telling me first."

Both siblings nodded solemnly.

"Alright then," Grandma said, her voice softening a bit. "Let's not waste any more time." She marched to the study and picked up the phone, ready to alert the authorities.

Grandma dialed a number she seemed to know by heart. After a moment, she spoke:

"Hello, Inspector? It's Grandma Diouf... Yes, good evening to you too. I'm afraid this isn't a social call... Remember those grandchildren of mine you were so impressed with? Well, they've done it."

She paused, listening.

"Yes, that's right. They've found your counterfeiters... At the old power plant by the Cazamoun River. They're there right now, printing fake money as we speak."

Another pause.

"How quickly can you get a team there?... Half an hour? That's good. We can't let them slip away."

She nodded, absorbing more information.

"You're sending three of your agents and those two Secret Service men?... Perfect. They're already in town, you say? Even better."

Grandma's voice took on a note of urgency, then shifted to a dry, sarcastic tone.

"Please hurry, Inspector. And while you're at it, could you perhaps arrest my grandchildren too? For driving their poor grandmother to an early grave with their mischiefs? »

She chuckled, then added more seriously, "And... thank you for taking them seriously."

She hung up and turned to Boubou and Aya, who were trying not to laugh.

"They'll have a team out there in half an hour," she told them. "Three special agents and two Secret Service men who've been working on this case are in town. Will that be enough?"

"Wow, Grandma! You sure know people!" Aya's eyes were as big as saucers.

Grandma continued, looking a bit proud. "Remember that government man who called me? He knew about your knack for solving mysteries. He said if you could find something real in this case, he'd officially recognize your detective skills—"

"Really?" Aya squeaked, hardly believing it.

"Yes. The inspector knew there was no stopping you two. He said you were just like your father. Looks like he was right. So I called him like he asked me if you found out anything new," Grandma explained, her eyes twinkling.

Boubou and Aya felt so proud. They were real detectives now, just like their dad had been!

"But there are three bad guys," Boubou said, sounding a little worried.

"Don't worry, the team they're sending will be enough," Grandma reassured him. "Now, how did you two find their hideout at the old power plant?"

❖

Boubou and Aya took turns telling Grandma how they uncovered the counterfeiters' operation.

"It all started when we noticed weird lights at the old power plant late at night," Boubou began.

Aya chimed in, "Yeah, and there were these strange men coming and going at odd hours."

"We tried asking around town, but nobody knew anything," Boubou continued. "So we decided to check it out ourselves."

"The first time we went, this really creepy guy chased us off," Aya said, shuddering at the memory. "He had this scary scar on his face and yelled at us to stay away."

Grandma frowned, but Boubou quickly added, "But that just made us more curious, Grandma! We knew something fishy was going on."

"So tonight, we snuck in through a broken window," Aya explained, her eyes wide with excitement. "And that's when we saw them, Grandma! They had this big machine, and it was printing fake money!"

"We could smell the ink and everything," Boubou added. "There were stacks of bills everywhere!"

Just as they were getting to the most exciting part—how they managed to escape without getting caught—they were interrupted by the sound of tires screeching to a halt right outside their house. The sudden noise made them all jump.

CHAPTER TWENTY FIVE

The Raid

"THE POLICE ARE HERE," GRANDMA DIOUF ANNOUNCED, HER voice filled with anticipation. "Let's go meet them."

They stepped outside to greet the officer on the front steps. A uniformed man hurried towards the house. Grandma Diouf spoke quietly, her voice barely above a whisper, "They're working out of the old power plant on the Cazamoun River. You know how to get there, right?"

The officer looked puzzled. "Can't say I do. Not by car, anyway."

Boubou jumped in, his eyes lighting up with excitement. "No worries! Here's what you do: follow the shore road, then turn onto this old loop. It's pretty empty now, but it goes right past where the old power plant used to be before they built the new road."

The officer scratched his head, trying to picture the route. "Oh, I think I remember now. The abandoned road, right?"

"You sure you can find it without getting lost?" Aya asked with concern and eagerness.

The officer thought for a moment, then his face brightened. "I've got an idea. Why don't you two come along and show us the way? It'll be faster, and we'll have a better chance of catching those guys."

He glanced at Grandma Diouf for permission, but Aya and Boubou were already buzzing with excitement.

"We're in!" Aya chirped, her eyes sparkling as she hopped into the vehicle.

Boubou, always thinking ahead, added, "Maybe we should park the car a little way from the plant and walk the rest. That way, we can sneak up on them."

Everyone nodded in agreement. They piled into the car, joining the other officers who looked tough and determined, their eyes alert in the moonlight that glinted off their badges.

The car zoomed through the cool night, racing along the shore road. The lights of Zinguichou twinkled behind them like tiny stars. Soon, they turned onto an old, forgotten path. The car bounced and bumped over the uneven ground, making everyone inside feel like they were on a rollercoaster.

As they got close to where Boubou and Aya had left their bikes earlier, the kids waved at the driver to stop. The car slowed down and came to a gentle halt.

They all got out, gathering in a small group under the big, bright moon. Officer Moussa took charge, his voice calm but full of authority. He quickly explained the plan, his words as sharp and clear as the moonlight around them.

"We'll follow this path until we reach the open space between the trees and the old power plant," Officer Moussa said, pointing to the dark shapes in the distance. "Team A will sneak around to the back of the plant. Team B and our backup will go straight to the front."

Everyone nodded, understanding what they needed to do. The air buzzed with excitement, like right before a big game. Each person was ready to play their part in the night's adventure. The moon shone down on them, making everything look magical and mysterious.

Boubou's eyes sparkled with excitement. Aya fidgeted with nervous energy, both thrilled and scared at the same time.

Officer Moussa turned to the kids with a serious look. "Remember, you two stay close to me. No wandering off, okay?"

They both nodded eagerly, feeling like real detectives on a top-secret mission.

❖

The moonlight cast long shadows as Officer Moussa led his team through the trees. Boubou and Aya crept alongside, their eyes wide with excitement. The old power plant loomed ahead, a dark shape against the star-speckled sky.

"This way," Boubou whispered, pointing to a narrow path. "There's also an old door around the back."

Officer Moussa nodded, signaling the team to follow. The soft earth muffled their footsteps, and the only sound was the occasional rustle of leaves in the night breeze.

Aya's heart raced as they drew closer to the plant. She tugged on Officer Moussa's sleeve. "There's a hole in the roof up there," she breathed, barely audible. "That's where we got in."

The officer's eyebrows rose, impressed.

As they neared the power plant, the air seemed to thicken with tension. Boubou felt like he could almost reach out and touch it. He glanced at Aya, saw the determination in her eyes, and knew she felt it too.

Officer Moussa raised his hand, bringing the group to a halt. They crouched in the shadows, the power plant now clearly visible. Lights flickered inside, confirming their suspicions. Someone was definitely home.

"Remember," Officer Moussa breathed, his voice barely a whisper, "stay close and stay quiet. This is where it gets dangerous."

Boubou and Aya nodded, their faces a mix of nerves and excitement. They were really doing this. They were part of a real police raid.

Officer Moussa gathered everyone close, his voice a low whisper that barely disturbed the night air.

"Alright, team. This is it. We split up now."

He pointed to a group of officers. "Team A, circle around back. Boubou mentioned an old service entrance. Use it."

The officers nodded, their faces set with determination. They melted into the shadows, moving with practiced stealth.

"Team B, with me. We'll take the front."

Boubou and Aya exchanged excited glances. Officer Moussa turned to them, his expression serious but kind.

"You two stick to me like glue, got it? No wandering off, no matter what happens."

"Yes, sir," they whispered in unison, hearts pounding.

As Team B spread out, preparing to approach the main entrance, Aya tugged on Boubou's sleeve.

"Look," she breathed, pointing to a high window. A faint light flickered inside, casting eerie shadows.

Boubou nodded, a chill running down his spine. "They're in there alright."

Officer Moussa overheard them. "Good eye, kids. That's valuable intel."

He spoke into his radio, voice barely above a whisper. "Team A, we have visual confirmation. Upper floor, west side. Proceed with caution."

Static crackled softly. "Copy that. In position."

The air seemed to crackle with tension. Boubou could feel his pulse in his ears. Aya's fingers were crossed so tightly they were turning white.

This was it. The moment they'd been waiting for. The raid was about to begin, and they were right in the middle of it.

Officer Moussa crouched behind a rusted oil drum, his team spread out in a semicircle around the power plant's main entrance. Boubou and Aya huddled close, barely daring to breathe.

The officer raised his hand, three fingers extended. Boubou felt his heart skip a beat. This was it.

Three… Officer Moussa's ring finger lowered.

Two… His middle finger followed.

One…

Just as his index finger was about to drop, a twig snapped somewhere in the darkness. Everyone froze.

Aya's eyes widened in panic. Had they been spotted? She glanced at Boubou, who looked equally terrified.

Officer Moussa held perfectly still, listening intently. Seconds stretched like hours.

Finally, a night bird called, breaking the silence. The officer's shoulders relaxed slightly. False alarm.

Officer Moussa locked eyes with Boubou and Aya and gave them a reassuring nod. Then, he turned back to the plant, raising his hand once more.

This time, there were no interruptions. As his last finger lowered, he whispered into his radio, "Go, go, go."

The response came immediately, barely a breath in the night. "Copy. Moving in."

For a heartbeat, nothing happened. The power plant loomed before them, silent and dark.

Then, chaos erupted.

❖

The front door burst open with a thunderous crash. At the same moment, the sound of shattering glass came from the back of the building.

Shouts filled the air. Flashlight beams cut through the darkness like lightning.

"Police! Don't move!"

Boubou and Aya watched, wide-eyed, as officers swarmed into the building. It was like a perfectly choreographed dance, each member knowing exactly where to go and what to do.

Officer Moussa turned to them, his face serious. "Stay close. Things are about to get hectic."

With that, he stood and rushed forward, Boubou and Aya right on his heels. The raid was in full swing, and they were heading straight into the heart of it.

The power plant erupted into chaos as the police raid began. Shouts and the crash of breaking glass filled the air as officers swarmed into the building from all sides.

Boubou and Aya, hiding behind Officer Moussa, watched wide-eyed as the scene unfolded like an action movie. Flashlight beams cut through the dusty air, revealing startled faces and ancient machinery.

Suddenly, Mako's desperate voice rang out above the commotion. "Nobody moves!"

All eyes turned to see the master forger grab Kirabo roughly by the arm. The boy's eyes were wide with terror as Mako dragged him towards a narrow staircase.

"I'm taking the kid to the roof!" Mako shouted, his voice edged with panic. "Anyone follows, and he goes over the edge!"

Before anyone could react, Mako was bounding up the steps, hauling a stumbling Kirabo behind him.

"No!" Aya cried out, her heart racing.

Officer Moussa sprang into action, barking orders to his team. As the officers scrambled to respond, Boubou tugged urgently on the officer's sleeve.

"We know the way to the roof!" he said. "Let us help!"

Officer Moussa hesitated for a split second, then nodded. "Alright, but stay behind me. Understood?"

Boubou nodded vigorously, falling in line behind the officer as they raced towards the stairs. But Aya had other ideas.

In the chaos, Aya's quick mind raced back to their earlier visit to the power plant. There was another way up – the old oak tree they'd used to climb onto the roof.

As Boubou and Officer Moussa turned towards the stairs, Aya made her move. She darted towards a side door, her heart pounding.

"Aya, stop!" Officer Moussa called out, spotting her sudden movement. "Come back here!"

But Aya was too quick. She slipped through the door and into the cool night air, the officer's shout fading behind her.

Officer Moussa hesitated, torn between pursuing Aya and chasing after Mako. "Boubou, where is she going?" he asked urgently.

"The oak tree!" Boubou replied, his eyes wide. "We used to climb it to get on the roof!"

Officer Moussa's face tightened with concern. "We can't let her go alone. Come on!"

As they raced after Aya, she was already sprinting across the shadowy grounds towards the familiar oak tree, its branches stretching towards the starry sky. Without hesitation, she began to climb, her hands finding the familiar holds in the rough bark.

She moved quickly and quietly, driven by the urgent need to help Kirabo. Behind her, she could hear Officer Moussa and Boubou calling her name, their voices filled with worry and frustration.

The power plant echoed with the sound of pounding feet and shouted orders. On the ground floor, Team A had cornered Uncle Dogo. The forger's shoulders slumped in defeat as an officer snapped handcuffs around his wrists, securing him to a massive generator.

"One down," an officer called out. "After Mako!"

Without missing a beat, the team raced towards the stairs, their flashlights bobbing in the darkness as they pursued the master forger and his young hostage.

Outside, Officer Moussa and Boubou burst through the side door, their eyes scanning the shadowy grounds.

"There!" Boubou shouted, pointing to a figure scrambling up the old oak tree.

Officer Moussa cupped his hands around his mouth. "Aya! Come down immediately! It's too dangerous!"

But Aya was already halfway up, her small form disappearing into the leaves.

"We have to go after her," Boubou insisted, tugging on the officer's sleeve.

Officer Moussa nodded grimly. "You're right. Let's go."

They sprinted to the base of the tree. Officer Moussa grabbed a low-hanging branch and tried to hoist himself up, but the branch creaked ominously under his weight.

"It's no use," he grunted, dropping back down. "We're too heavy. The branches won't hold us."

Boubou's face fell as he realized the officer was right. They were stuck on the ground, helpless to stop Aya from putting herself in danger.

Up on the roof, Mako had run out of options. The cool night air whipped around him as he backed towards the edge, his eyes wild with desperation. The ancient power plant's roof creaked ominously under his feet, rust-covered pipes and old ventilation units casting long shadows in the moonlight.

Officers poured out of the stairwell and through the roof's hole like a flood, their boots scraping against the gritty rooftop. They emerged from the dark opening one after another, spreading out across the roof with practiced efficiency. Flashlight beams crisscrossed the darkness, illuminating a scene of heart-stopping tension. The lights danced across Mako's sweat-slicked face, highlighting the fear and determination in his eyes.

"Freeze! Let the boy go!" an officer shouted, his voice almost lost in the wind that howled around the building.

Mako's grip on Kirabo tightened, causing the boy to let out a frightened whimper. Kirabo's feet dangled precariously over the edge, nothing but empty air between him and the hard ground far below. His small hands clutched desperately at Mako's arm, knuckles white with terror.

"Stay back!" Mako's voice cracked, a mixture of panic and anger. "I swear, I'll drop him! Don't test me!"

The officers formed a semicircle, their weapons trained on Mako but fingers hovering uncertainly over triggers. One wrong move could send Kirabo plummeting to his death.

Time seemed to stretch like taffy, each second an eternity of suspense. The only sounds were the wind's mournful howl, Kirabo's soft sobs, and the rapid breathing of everyone on the roof.

In the tense standoff, no one noticed the small figure slowly emerging from the branches of the old oak tree.

Mako's desperation grew with each passing second. "I mean it!" he shouted, his voice cracking. "One more step and the kid goes over!"

Kirabo whimpered, tears streaming down his face. His feet dangled precariously over the edge, toes barely scraping the roof's surface.

Down below, Officer Moussa squinted up at the roof, his mind racing. Suddenly, his eyes widened in realization. "Boubou," he whispered, "I think I know what Aya's planning."

Without taking his eyes off the roof, Officer Moussa raised his radio to his lips. "All units on the roof, listen carefully. Keep Mako's attention focused on you. Whatever happens, do not look towards the old oak tree. Repeat, do not look at the tree."

Confused acknowledgments crackled through the radio.

Up on the roof, Aya had shimmied out onto a thick branch overhanging the edge. Her heart pounded as she inched forward, the branch bowing slightly under her weight.

Mako, oblivious to the danger behind him, continued his threats. "I'll do it! Don't think I won't!"

As the officers kept Mako distracted with tense negotiations, Aya took a deep breath. It was now or never.

In one fluid motion, she swung down from the branch, her small hands grasping Kirabo's shoulders. With a strength born of desperation, she yanked the boy from Mako's grasp.

Kirabo let out a startled yelp as he suddenly found himself swinging through the air, Aya's arms wrapped tightly around him.

Mako spun around, his face a mask of shock. "What the—"

But it was too late. Aya and Kirabo were already swinging back towards the safety of the tree, the branch creaking under their combined weight.

As they disappeared into the thick foliage, a cheer erupted from the officers on the roof. Mako, realizing his leverage was gone, slumped to his knees in defeat.

"It's over, Mako," an officer said, stepping forward with handcuffs at the ready. "Surrender now."

With a bitter laugh, Mako raised his hands above his head. His eyes, cold and calculating, swept across the officers surrounding him. "Well, well," he sneered. "You may have won this round, but don't think for a second this is over."

An officer approached, handcuffs at the ready. Mako's lips curled into a sinister smile. "You have no idea how deep this goes, do you?" he hissed. "I'm just the tip of the iceberg."

As the cuffs clicked shut around his wrists, Mako leaned in close to the officer. "Watch your back," he whispered. "My associates don't take kindly to interference. And they're everywhere."

The officer tried to maintain his composure. "Save it for the judge, Mako. Your threats don't scare us."

Mako chuckled darkly. "Oh, but they should. You think locking me up will end this? You've just made some very powerful enemies, my friend. Sleep tight."

As they led him towards the roof exit, Mako glanced back at the tree where Aya and Kirabo had disappeared. His eyes narrowed. "And those kids," he growled. "They'd better watch out. In my world, we don't forget… and we don't forgive."

The first officer gave him a rough shove. "That's enough out of you. Let's go."

As they disappeared through the roof access, an uneasy silence fell over the remaining officers. One turned to another, his voice low. "You don't think he's serious, do you?"

His colleague shrugged, trying to hide his discomfort. "Who knows? But something tells me this isn't the last we've heard of Mako and his gang."

The master forger's reign of crime had come to an end, but his chilling words lingered in the air, a stark reminder that sometimes, catching the villain is just the beginning of a much bigger story.

❖

As the officers led Mako towards the waiting police car, his eyes locked with Aya's for a brief, intense moment. The master forger's gaze was a mixture of begrudging respect and veiled threat, sending a chill down Aya's spine despite her triumph.

"Well, I'll be a counterfeit coin," Mako muttered. "Outsmarted by a pint-sized monkey swinger."

Officer Moussa opened the car door, his badge gleaming in the moonlight. "Don't worry, Mako. Where you're going, you'll have plenty of time to branch out into new hobbies." he quipped, unable to resist.

Mako rolled his eyes. "Really? I've printed better jokes on fake money."

As he settled into the backseat, Mako's eyes narrowed. "Don't get too comfortable, kids," he called out to Aya and Boubou. "In my world, we have long memories… and longer reaches."

Officer Moussa slammed the door shut, cutting off Mako's ominous words. "That's enough out of you," he growled, then turned to his fellow officers. "Let's get him to the station. I think we've all had enough excitement for one night."

As the car drove off, one agent turned to Officer Moussa. "You know, I think I'm going to like this town. The criminals might be crafty, but our local kids? They're the real masterminds."

They all looked at Boubou and Aya with a mixture of pride and concern, the weight of Mako's veiled threat hanging in the air.

*　*　*

CHAPTER TWENTY SIX

The Reckoning

THE NEXT DAY, WHEN THE FULL STORY OF THE MONEY-MAKING gang came out, Zinguichou was buzzing with excitement. Everyone was talking about how the Diouf siblings had busted one of the most dangerous groups that had ever outsmarted the government.

After catching Uncle Dogo and his partners in crime, Boubou, Aya, and the Secret Service agents didn't waste a second. Boubou remembered something important - the address in Zakar where the mysterious Jango lived. He'd overheard Uncle Dogo mention it earlier.

"Quick! We need to send a message to the Zakar police," Boubou said, his eyes wide with urgency.

Aya raised an eyebrow. "Look at you, bossing around the government task force. Getting a taste for power, big brother?"

But their quick thinking paid off. The Zakar police arrested Jango, who turned out to be the mastermind behind the whole operation. He was the one who had planned how to spread the fake money around.

"It's like a spider web," Aya mused. "And we just caught the big, sneaky spider in the middle!"

The police didn't stop there. They rounded up the crooks in Zabrousse and Zinguichou, including the shifty woman in black who had given Boubou and Aya so much trouble.

Later, Grandma Diouf gathered her grandchildren to explain what they'd uncovered.

"You won't believe this," she said, her eyes twinkling with pride. "The machinery in that old power plant? It was top-notch stuff. The best money could buy - or in this case, make!"

Boubou leaned in, fascinated. "But how did they make the fake money look so real?"

"Well," Grandma continued, "it turns out Mako used to be an expert at making printing plates. He created the engravings that let them copy our currency so perfectly. Uncle Dogo and the others helped print the bills."

Aya couldn't help but interrupt. "So Mako was like an evil artist? Picasso, but for paper?"

Grandma chuckled. "Something like that. He made sure they had the right paper too. And get this - when we raided their hideout, there were enough fake bills on the table to add up to almost fifty thousand dollars!"

"Whoa," Boubou whispered, his eyes as big as saucers.

"Yeah," Aya added with a smirk. "Talk about making money grow on trees!"

Thanks to the officers' speedy work, every single member of the gang was caught. No one slipped through their net. In Mako's room, they found a notebook filled with names and addresses. It was like a treasure map of crime, showing all the people who helped spread the fake money across the country.

"It's like they gift-wrapped their whole operation for us," Aya quipped, shaking her head in disbelief.

By the next day, every last person on that list was in handcuffs.

❖

The day after the big bust, the two Secret Service agents who helped catch the counterfeiters at the old power plant paid a special visit to the Diouf home. They wanted to congratulate Boubou and Aya in person.

As the agents walked up to the house, Boubou straightened his shirt, trying to look important. "Look, Aya. The big-shot agents are here. Think they'll offer us jobs?"

Aya snorted. "In your dreams, little brother. Though I suppose they might need someone to fetch their coffee."

"We've been snooping around for a week trying to catch these guys," said one of the agents, "but we never thought to check the old power plant. What made you suspicious of that place?"

Boubou explained how they first learned about strangers taking over the power plant and their initial visit.

"To be honest," he said, "I got suspicious when Uncle Dogo offered us a reward for helping save Kirabo from the river. He pulled out two fifty-dollar bills and tried to give them to us. Then the other guy snatched them away, turned around, and later offered them to us again."

The Secret Service agent grinned. "Uncle Dogo tried to give you fake money, and his buddy Mako was worried you'd figure it out and trace it back to them."

"I guess so. But it made me wonder what was up. After that, Aya and I kept an eye on the place. Everything seemed fishy, so we decided to investigate."

"And boy, are we glad you did! That was some smart detective work, and I promise the government won't forget it."

True to the agent's word, before the month was out, the Diouf siblings received a $1,000 check as a reward for helping catch the counterfeiters.

"Enough money," Adama Sambou joked when he heard about it, "to keep that motorboat of yours running for a couple of years, at least!"

As for Uncle Dogo and his gang, they all got long prison sentences. Boubou and Aya were especially concerned about Kirabo, so they asked their Grandmother to make sure the boy would be okay. Mrs. Diouf's efforts revealed that "Uncle Dogo" wasn't Kirabo's uncle at all, but a sneaky criminal who had taken him from an orphanage, planning to raise him as a future partner in crime.

Hearing about Kirabo's situation, a kind-hearted citizen of Zinguinchou offered to give him a home and send him to school. The Diouf siblings were thrilled that Kirabo would have a chance at a better life.

"We'll take you out on our motorboat sometime, Kirabo," they promised him.

His face lit up. "Really? That'd be awesome!"

"Of course! You're one of the gang now."

"Will you take me along next time you go detectiving?" Kirabo asked eagerly.

"When we go what?" Aya laughed.

"Detectiving! You know, being detectives and stuff."

The Diouf siblings chuckled. "Oh, right! We'll see, Kirabo. But chances are we won't have any detective work for a while. It's not every day that counterfeiters set up shop in Zinguinchou, you know," Boubou said.

"And thank goodness for that!" Aya added.

Little did the Diouf siblings know that more adventures awaited them, where they'd get to show off their detective skills just like they did at the old power plant.

When they went to cash their reward check, they brought along Adama, Kirabo, Pierre, Amath, Djily, and Bouma. The Diouf siblings had promised to celebrate by treating everyone to ice cream, followed by a motorboat race where Pierre would try once again to beat their boat, the Mystery, with his own boat.

"I think $20 should cover it," said Boubou, handing the check to the bank teller. "We can use the rest for boat fuel."

"So you want to deposit $980?" the teller asked.

"That's right."

The teller handed over two $10 bills. Adama Sambou grabbed one, pretended to bite it, and stared at the ceiling for a moment before giving it back to Boubou.

"Looks real to me," he said with a wink. "But you can never be too careful these days, what with all this funny money going around!"

END OF VOLUME 3

BOUBOU AND AYA WILL RETURN IN

"THE KIDNAPPER'S PLAN"

About The Author

Walter Simin is a character. He is a multifaceted author and artist, renowned for his work as a director in film and television, his captivating narratives in children's literature and his evocative paintings exhibited worldwide. With a career that has spanned across Africa for over a decade, Walter embodies a vast African soul in both his literary and artistic endeavors. His diverse background, rich with global experiences, deeply influences his storytelling, infusing his works with authenticity and a broad cultural perspective.

As a father of four and a devoted husband and dog owner, Walter's life is a vibrant blend of family, creativity, and exploration. His debut series, "Boubou & Aya," was inspired by his desire to write adventure books for a friend's son who had lost his mother. Through these stories, Walter aims to help children who have lost parents stay connected with them through imagination, adventure, and magic, showing that their loved ones are still there to guide and support them always. This series is a testament to his ability to weave tales that resonate with both the innocence of childhood and the profound depth of African heritage, while also addressing sensitive emotional experiences.

Beyond writing, Walter's artistic talent extends to the canvas, where his passion for vibrant colors and bold textures translates into stunning paintings that have garnered acclaim in art circles around the world. His work, both as an author and an artist, reflects his profound connection to the African continent, its culture, and its people, making him a unique and compelling voice in the realms of both literature and art.

A FAVOR BEFORE YOU GO...

As we close this volume of « The Adventures Of Boubou & Aya » I hope you enjoyed this journey as much as I loved creating it. Your companionship through these pages has been invaluable.

Now, I have a small but significant request. If you found yourself captivated by the mysteries of Boubou and Aya's world, please leave a review. Whether it's a few words or a detailed account of your experience, your thoughts mean the world to authors like myself, and your feedback helps other readers discover and join in on our adventures.

You can leave your thoughts wherever you purchased the book on your favourite review site, or directly on the book page on Amazon.

Thank you for being a part of this journey, and I can't wait to share more adventures with you in the future!

With heartfelt thanks,

Walter Simin

WANT TO GET SOCIAL?

Let's keep in touch! Connect with me here:

www.waltersimin.com

Facebook: waltersiminbooks
Instagram: @waltersimin
Tiktok: @waltersimin

www.ingramcontent.com/pod-product-compliance
Lightning Source LLC
LaVergne TN
LVHW031323190726
843493LV00013B/3029